FAMILIAR TERRITORY

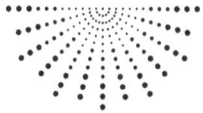

SAM CHEEVER

ELECTRIC PROSE PUBLICATIONS

Independence is the most important thing to LA...but can she live with herself if her freedom ends up costing her family their lives?

She'd watched a friend succumb to the smothering control of another magical user. She'd made a promise to herself it would never happen to her. For centuries her family has worn the badge of Familiar proudly, serving a long line of powerful Witches and becoming as formidable as the ones they served. But LA doesn't believe she needs a Familiar alliance to be strong.

Until people she cares about begin disappearing... turning up dead.

Until a powerful and handsome male Witch walks into her life and forges an inadvertent magic bond while trying to save her life.

Now she finds herself in exactly the position she never wanted. But she quickly realizes she can't save her friends and family alone. So it comes down to losing her independence or watching everyone she cares about die.

Will LA find a way to keep her independence and still save the people she cares about most? Or will her burning need for freedom be the cause of their deaths?

CHAPTER ONE

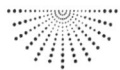

he stupid cat was going to be the death of me.

He crouched beneath a rusted out cabinet and hissed whenever I moved. Every time I spoke to the bedraggled creature it spat at me and backed more deeply into the shadows underneath the cabinet. All I could see was the glow of his large green eyes. Beautiful eyes. Just about the only attractive thing about the ugly critter.

Including his personality.

"Come on, buddy. I promise I only want to help."

The cat yowled fervently, ending the long complaint with a hiss that promised me pain if I tried to get any closer.

I sighed my frustration, sitting back on my heels to think. I'd been chasing the recalcitrant feline for almost a week, and I'd been unable to lure it out with any of my usual tricks. The difficult creature had already snubbed kibble, tuna, even a can of delectable anchovies I'd dug out of the back of my pantry. I was at a loss. He didn't seem in the least inclined to let me "save" him.

I had only one last option and I was reluctant to use it. It was too easy and way too tempting. But it was starting to look like I wasn't going to have a choice.

Standing up, I quickly glanced around to make sure I wasn't being watched. The fenced-in lot was empty except for me and the cat, and the street beyond the fence was quiet. Most of my neighbors were already at work, and the ones who weren't were probably still asleep.

The coast was clear.

But was my conscience?

I eyed the cat and earned another hiss for my trouble. That hiss twanged my last nerve. "Okay, fuzzface. That's it. You and I need to have a meeting of the minds."

The cat moved slightly forward as if drawn by my angry tones. I was surprised, but then the animal hadn't done anything I expected so far. It made a twisted kind of sense that he would continue to catch me off guard.

I gave it one more second's thought and then made my decision. The cat watched me as I walked to a spot several feet away and sat down, crossing my legs and spreading my hands on my knees.

The feline's intelligent green gaze was filled with anticipation, as if he knew what I was about to do. I don't know how. Even I wasn't entirely sure if I was actually going through with it. I only knew I needed to do something or the cat underneath the cabinet would be lost.

So I closed my eyes and focused my thoughts inward, searching for the core of energy that pulsed in my breast. My tentative exploration was all too eagerly received. As I'd feared, the magic flared toward my tentative touch and grabbed hold, surging outward far too fast.

I panicked and clamped it down, gritting my teeth as

the energy tried to break free. I barely managed to wrestle the magic back so I could control it. When I opened my eyes again I gave a yelp of surprise.

The cat was sitting right in front of me, its wide green eyes narrowed. I clasped my throat. "You scared me half to death." I smiled. "But I'm glad you showed up so I didn't need to use…well…you don't care about that, do you?"

The cat stared at me another moment and then, when I reached for it, growled and slashed at my hand, ripping several long slices across the back.

"Ow!"

He leapt into the air and took off. Before I could even move, the critter had scampered through the gate I'd apparently forgotten to latch, and disappeared.

"Dammit!" Jumping to my feet, I cradled my bleeding hand, briefly considering trying to go after him. But I couldn't even see the damnable creature anymore and I had no idea where to look.

"Are you all right?"

For the second time in moments I jumped in surprise. I swung around to find a tall man with dark, nearly black hair coming through the gate.

"I'm sorry to interrupt…" He swung his hands around as if to indicate the area. "…whatever you're doing here. But I heard you cry out." His dark silver gaze slid to my hand. "You're hurt."

I covered my hand and pulled my pride around me like a shield. "I'm fine." Starting toward the gate, I gave the sexy stranger a wide berth, determined to keep my distance. Unfortunately, he reached out and snagged my wrist before I could move past. Electricity surged between us, spitting from our fingertips and merging over our hands in a silvery-blue arc. A jagged volt of energy sliced through me, causing the magic at my core to flare painfully to life.

To my horror, my cheeks started to sting and my fingernails burned.

His gaze shot to mine and held. For just the briefest instant, I thought I saw something feral move through the silvery depths but it quickly slid away.

In a panic, I jerked away from his touch, all but running for the gate. He called out to me but I kept going. Whatever he was, I didn't like the way he'd affected me and I was going to make sure it never happened again. I didn't even slow until I reached the shabby, careworn brownstone I called home. Diving through the front door, I slammed it shut and locked it, leaning against the cool wood surface as I tried to calm my pounding heart.

What had just happened?

Had I really joined energy with a perfect stranger?

The implications made my stomach tighten with dread. Shaking my head, I pushed away from the door and hurried through the house to the sanctuary in the back. I'd lose myself in work...forget all about the husky-voiced hottie with the intense, silver gaze.

What had happened between us was just static electricity. Nothing more.

That was my story and I was going to cling to it with everything I had. Because the alternative was too terrifying to contemplate.

~

AN HOUR LATER, as I was cleaning out a large kennel filled

with soiled newspaper shreds and spilled food, my phone rang.

I pulled my cell from my pocket and looked at the ID, hitting the *Answer* button. "Hey, Mom."

"Peaches. How are you?"

Judging from the probing quality of her voice, I realized it wasn't a throwaway question. "I'm fine. Why?"

"It's just...well...I felt something a while ago. Something shifted in your universe."

Closing my eyes, I fought for calm, understanding that my mother, one of the strongest Familiars I knew, would hear any sign of stress in my tone. "I've been trying to catch this stray cat..."

"No. It's something else. What happened, LA?"

Biting back a groan, I tried again to throw her off the scent. "No really, this cat has really been stressing me out."

"LA, if that cat doesn't want to be caught you should respect its wishes. You of all people should understand that."

"I know, but it's so skinny and looks so sick. I'm really afraid it doesn't have long to live."

"You run a sanctuary, Peaches, not a prison ward. Respect the cat's desire to die on its own terms."

She was right. I knew that. But it was killing me. "I know. You're right."

"Now tell me what really happened."

Sighing, I rubbed a hand over my eyes, suddenly oh so weary. "It was nothing."

"Trust me when I tell you it was something."

"The cat scratched me..."

"Yes?"

"And this guy asked me if I was all right."

Silence beat through the phone lines and I wanted to scream. She was doing exactly what I knew she'd do... assuming the encounter was important somehow. "It was just a guy."

"What happened between you?"

The woman was a Pitbull and she had my life firmly between her teeth, jerking fiercely. She wouldn't stop tugging until I told her what she wanted to hear. "He was just worried about my bleeding hand. That's all."

"LeeAnn Kristin Mapes..."

Oh gawd! Not the full name thing. "It was just static electricity!" I shouted into the phone in desperation.

Unfortunately there was no missing the huge gasp from the other end of the line. "You've found him!"

My head was shaking even before she finished the sentence. "I didn't find anybody..."

"You finally found your Witch, LA."

"I haven't found anything of the sort..."

"What does he look like? Is he handsome?"

I scrunched up my nose. "What difference does that make?"

"It makes no difference, but it doesn't hurt if he's cute."

Rolling my eyes, I looked down as a sleek black cat slipped along my calf. "He's very cute. Does that make you happy?"

"Oh, yes!" She actually giggled. I thought I might puke. "I have to call your grandmother."

Seeing a way out of the current conversation I eagerly agreed. "Okay, I'll talk to you lat..."

"Go see him right now and tell him you'll do it."

My eyes went wide. "Do *it*?" Good god, don't let my mother be telling me to have sex with a perfect stranger.

6

My psyche would be permanently dented. I'd never recover.

"Offer your Familiar services. If he needs references let me know. I have a whole binder full of them."

"I don't even know if he's a Witch."

"When you touched, electricity arched between you, correct?"

I frowned, unwilling to verify the event for her. "Mom…"

"Your magic flared didn't it? You sprouted whiskers and claws?"

"No, I…"

"LA, stop denying reality. It's not healthy. And denying your birthright is even less healthy. Go talk to your Witch and make your blood pact. Now I have to speak to your grandmother. There are many plans to make. We'll have to have the joining ceremony at Grandmama's house. This place is under construction…"

"No, Mom…" But it was no use, I was suddenly talking to air as my mother disconnected, off to run my life for me since obviously I was unable to run it correctly myself.

If the doorbell hadn't rung in that moment I might have been able to sit down and figure out a way out of my predicament. But its insistent blaring through the brownstone was impossible to ignore.

And the person waiting for me on the other side was dangerous to my sanity.

CHAPTER TWO

*T*he demon standing on my doorstep was the epitome of dangerous. His dark hair shone with blue light as if burnished by the sun, though the day beyond my door was overcast with a coming storm. His midnight gaze flashed and smoldered as he gave me a predatory smile and I steeled myself against his poisonous charm, knowing from experience how vulnerable I was to it. "Hello, lovely." Brock's sexy English accent only added to his deadly charm, but it was far from necessary for him to beguile. All he needed to do for that was stand there.

"Brock. What can I do for you?" Even as I said the words I cringed inwardly. It wasn't like me to give him an opening like that. Apparently the morning's events had taken more out of me than I'd realized.

He leaned closer without even appearing to move. The dark-eyed demon let his gaze heat as it skimmed over me, making me feel undressed. "I'm glad you asked." And he really was, because full demons were just below Familiars in the hierarchy, as destined to serve us as we were destined to serve the Witches.

Not for the first time, I wondered if that destiny rubbed Brock the wrong way as it did me.

I stepped backward to escape his heat. "I'm really busy. Did you need something?"

He chuckled huskily and I closed my eyes, knowing things weren't going to get better any time soon. "Let me rephrase that. Whatever you're here for, I'm not interested and I can't help. But hey," I grabbed the edge of the door. "Have a nice day."

He stopped the door with his foot and pushed inside, forcing me back. "I'm afraid this can't wait. I'm here at your grandmother's behest."

I barely kept from rolling my eyes. Celeste Mapes was an incredibly intelligent woman, even more powerful than my mother, and as charming and beautiful as she'd been at twenty, but where Brock Duarte was concerned, she had no more common sense than the stupid cat I'd been stalking that morning. "Celeste sent you?"

He inclined his head and suddenly he was standing wayyyy too close, the heat from his long body like the fires of Hell. "She did."

"Why?"

"We have a situation downtown."

"What kind of situation?"

"I really shouldn't tell you. This is Celeste's show…"

I grabbed the door and tried closing it again. Unfortunately there was a tall, impossibly annoying demon in the way. "Goodbye, demon."

He tipped his head, giving me a smile that made my

bones melt. "But since it's you and I have a weakness for your cranky, abrasive charm..."

"Brock..." I warned softly.

"Missing Familiars."

My eyes went wide. "More than one?"

"Many more. As near as we can tell there are a dozen magical souls missing from the shared web."

I frowned, suddenly realizing he was right. I'd felt the difference in the energy the last time I'd connected. Though I'd ignored it because I figured some of the missing were simply cloaking themselves. "Maybe they don't want to be found."

"Like that cat this morning?"

I blinked, a knot forming in my gut. "What do you know about the cat?"

"I know it wasn't just a cat."

I swore softly. On some level I'd known that too. "He was a shapeshifter."

"Yes. A Familiar. But he was scared and injured. He's running from something."

"Dangit," I murmured. "I should have seen it." The intelligent, probing gaze...the seeming ability to read my actions and anticipate how to avoid them. "You're right. That cat didn't want me to catch it."

"He doesn't know whom to trust."

In that moment I realized Brock knew more than he was telling me. "What's going on, demon?"

He turned away, heading toward the door. "I'm not at liberty to say." The annoying creature opened my front door and turned back, his perfectly sculpted lips curving upward. "Celeste needs to see you today. She told me to tell you not to even think about ignoring her summons. If you do she's perfectly fine with descending on your little sanctuary here." He stepped through the door. "And she won't come alone."

The door closed softly in his face without him even touching it. I swore again. Hopefully none of my neighbors saw his arrogant little display.

I shoved the worry back as bigger concerns flared in my mind.

I'd been summoned by the Queen of Familiars.

And I realized I'd rather bite my fingers off, one by one, than honor that summons.

THE SUN WAS BACK, turning the water that had gathered on the streets after the heavy rain into a muggy blanket. The humidity made the ninety-degree day almost intolerable. I pulled my elderly two-seater MG into the parking garage beneath my grandmother's office building and parked in a VIP slot near the elevator. It was one of the few perks I allowed myself that came as the result of my family's position. And I rarely took advantage of even that in my ongoing efforts to remain my own person, distant in every way from the calling that dogged the members of my family.

I usually didn't manage the feat as well as I would have liked. But I never stopped trying.

Persistence was yet another inherited trait I couldn't seem to deny.

Soft music played in the elevator as it shot to the top floor of the twenty story building. Though my grandmother owned the building and the business that built it,

Familiar, Inc. was housed on only the 18th and 19th floors. My grandmother and mother lived in the two apartments that made up the 20th.

I got off on the 19th floor and waved at the receptionist. "She's expecting me."

"Yes. Go on in, LA." The woman cocked a perfect dark gold eyebrow. "Good luck."

I would have liked to ask her what she was talking about but my grandmama's assistant chose that moment to poke his slick, black head out of her office. As usual, they'd felt my arrival in the area.

Damn the web.

"How are you, LA?" Jacob Withers asked. He pulled the door wide to usher me inside. "We haven't seen you around here for a while."

I didn't miss the subtle dig but chose to ignore it. "I'm good. Busy as usual."

He frowned a bit when I didn't do one of the two things he'd hoped for.

1. Take the bait and apologize for not being around or;
B. Ask him how he was doing.

Since he'd started off by being a jerk, I wasn't going to care how he was. Even if we *had* dated for a couple of very long years.

Two elegant women in feminine but business-like suits sat at a round glass table across the enormous office. They had their heads together and a pile of documents on the table between them. The sun shone through to gild their reddish blonde heads and turn their delicate features porcelain. Not for the first time, I wished I'd inherited some of the perks of being a woman in my family, instead of just all the annoying obligations. My own hair wasn't so much gilded by the sun as it was enflamed. And I couldn't seem to pull off the feminine suit thing. I pretty much looked like a box with legs in them.

My resemblance to my mom and grandmother also didn't include their proclivity for serving as Familiar to the Witch of their choosing. Or, in their case, several Witches each. With their advanced age...Mom was coming up on her first century and Celeste, in addition to being the founder and owner of *Familiar, Inc.* was nearly three hundred years young...they could pretty much pick any number of Witches to enhance with their magical charms.

I'd yet to pick a single Witch and fully intended never to saddle myself with that obligation.

Grandmama looked up and smiled. Her pale, peach lipstick perfectly matched the creamy color on her high cheeks and complimented the strawberry blonde of her hair. Her wide, blue-green eyes were filled with impatience, a look I saw mirrored in my mother's gaze when she looked up too. "Oh good, she's here." My mother lifted a hand and wiggled her fingers to indicate that I should join them.

Celeste shoved the pile of papers away and pointed toward a chair across from her. "Sit, child. We have much to discuss."

I couldn't imagine what that would be. I doubted they wanted to talk about the cost of bulk kitty litter or the recent outbreak of fleas in my sanctuary. "I don't have much time," I said before bending down and giving each perfectly coiffed woman a peck on a porcelain cheek.

Before I could stop myself, I ran a hand through my own more red than blonde locks, wishing I'd taken the time to brush my hair before coming inside. Driving with the top down in my little mudgie-bug was fun, but it wasn't exactly conducive to tidy hair.

"Nonsense," my mother told me. "You have all the time in the world. It's not as if those cats care about where you are."

I frowned, hating when she denigrated my work. "I know you don't think what I do is important, Mother…"

"Pshaw," she responded.

"We have more important things to discuss," Celeste said, interrupting us before we could indulge in the usual catfight. Complete with real fangs and claws.

I sat down, determinedly refusing to tug my cotton shirt straight or brush cat hair off my short skirt. "What's going on?"

"Didn't Brock tell you?"

I shrugged. "He was vague as usual. Just something about missing Familiars."

She sighed. "He's such a chore."

"Why don't you fire him," I asked reasonably.

"Because he's very good at what he does. And he's decidedly delicious."

My mother rolled her eyes. "Stop acting like a feline in heat, Celeste."

I barely suppressed a grin. Of all the things I loved about my grandmother, her brash honesty was my favorite. Love her or hate her, you always knew exactly where you stood.

Celeste winked at me. "I can forgive him for being a bit scattered on this one, LA. I'm afraid his little cousin, Tabitha is one of the missing Familiars."

I felt my eyes go wide. "Tabby? Oh no! How long has she been gone?"

"Three days. And she's just the latest in a string of missing Familiars."

"Any idea what's going on?"

My mother shook her head. "They haven't entirely disappeared from the web. Their life forces are still showing. But they're..." she frowned as if searching for the right word. "disconnected somehow."

"Faded," Celeste said on a nod. "I've never seen anything like it and, to tell you the truth, it has me a little unnerved."

"That's terrible," I said. "But I'm not sure what you want me to do about it."

Celeste held my gaze for a long moment and my stomach started to twist. Suddenly I knew exactly what she wanted me to do. I lifted my hands, shaking my head. "No."

"Yes, child. You owe it to your people."

"My people!" I screeched. "What people? The people who constantly denigrate me for my choices? The people who won't even speak to me unless they have to? Those people?"

Celeste stared hard at me for a long moment and then nodded. I knew in that moment that I was toast. "I'm sorry to hear Tabby was unkind to you."

I blinked, swallowed hard, and forced the words from my throat. "She wasn't. She's always been very kind to me, in fact. Unlike her cousin."

"We know how you feel about the family business, LA," my mom said softly. "If there was anyone else who could do what you do we'd ask them."

I arched a brow in disbelief. "There's nobody else?"

"No, child," Celeste told me. "No other Familiars. Tracking is a higher power. It's a skill generally held only by Witches."

I knew my secret talent was special among Familiars. I'd heard it often enough growing up. If I was being honest with myself, I'd have to admit that it was one of the reasons I resisted an alliance. If I could carry tracking magic just like a Witch, why would I subjugate myself to one? "Then why don't you just ask one of them to help? Surely somebody here has an alliance with a tracking Witch?"

My mother shook her head. "We need to keep this in house, LA. We don't know who we can trust. Since Familiars seem to be the targets, we have to assume the danger comes from outside our group."

I shook my head. "I'm sorry…"

Celeste lifted a single, slender eyebrow and held my gaze. She didn't speak. She didn't need to. I received the message loud and clear. Expelling a frustrated breath, I relented. "All right. I'll do it just this once. And just for Tabby."

Celeste smiled.

My mother grinned knowingly.

I quietly turned to flame beneath my skin. "I mean it. Just this once."

Celeste stood up and took my arm. "Of course, dear." She guided me to the door and stood back as I pulled it open. "Let me know what you find out."

I nodded, too angry to speak.

"Oh, and LA."

I stopped, my teeth grinding together as I reluctantly turned back.

"Say hello to your new Witch for me. Word on the street is that he's a phenomenal talent."

A loud creaking sound emerged and I forced my jaw to separate lest I fracture a tooth. Several things slid through my mind, all of them heartfelt and angry, but I didn't say any of them.

At that point I thought it was safer to make my escape before I said something we would all regret.

I stomped out of the office, ignoring the receptionist as she called out a hearty farewell.

Jacob was on the phone as I left and I gave him a quick wave as I headed toward the elevators, punching a button and fidgeting as I waited for it to arrive.

"Hello, LA."

I glanced up and saw a pretty Familiar coming toward me down the hall. She was clutching the hands of two small children. The little girl was the mirror image of her mother, with shiny brown curls and wide, light brown eyes. The boy had darker hair and deep-set hazel eyes. He stared at me almost angrily, and I blinked under his fierce regard. "Hey. How are you…?" I realized with a quick jolt of embarrassment that I'd forgotten her name.

"Holly," she said with a soft smile. "These are my kids, Lena and Kristofer."

"Hey, kids."

We stood for a moment in uncomfortable silence, both of us keenly aware that I should have known her name.

The elevator door dinged open and I let them precede me inside. As I punched the button for the first floor, I asked. "Is it take your kids to work day?" I gave her an apologetic smile and she returned it.

But there was concern in her gaze. "Something like that."

Giving her aura a quick perusal, I saw the tinge of purple at the edges. She was worried about something. "They're beautiful children."

"I'm not a child," Kristopher said angrily.

"Kristopher!" Holly cuffed him gently on the shoulder.

He rolled his eyes.

"He hates coming with me to work," Holly explained.

"It's so lame here."

I realized the kid had to be close to twelve. That explained the attitude. I would have liked to commiserate. I'd always hated being dragged to *Familiar, Inc* as a kid too. I'd pretty much hated everything about the Familiar world. "Sorry. Of course you're not."

He glared at me as if he thought I was being condescending and I gave up. The doors opened and I passed through. "It was nice seeing you, Holly." Hurrying toward the exit, I tried to ignore the feeling of relief swamping me as I plunged back out into the sunshine.

CHAPTER THREE

I drove much too fast on the way home, parking crookedly at the curb and slamming into my house. I flung my keys on the little half round table in the hall and stalked angrily back to the door, which hadn't quite latched when I slammed it into its frame.

A hand appeared between the frame and the door as I reached for it and I gave a little squeal.

The door opened wider and a handsome face popped through. The Good Samaritan Witch from up the street gave me a disarming smile.

Well, not quite disarming, but it did slow me down a little as my parts seized and my systems blue screened.

"Hello again."

I glared at him. "Do you not see this cranky look on my face?"

His smile widened. "I do actually. It's really pretty terrifying."

"And yet there you stand, seemingly unmoved."

He came the rest of the way through the door and

shoved his hands into his pockets, as if to show the skittish crazy lady that he meant no harm. "I understand the desire for independence."

I blinked. I had to admit, of all the things I'd expected him to say, that wasn't one of them. "What are you, some kind of self-help greeting card writer?"

He laughed. "No, it's just…"

"Then what are you doing here?" I knew I was being rude, but something ugly was driving me and I seemed unable to slam on the brakes.

He held up his hands. "I realize that being summoned before the Queen can't be fun."

"How the hell…"

He lifted his hands. "Full disclosure, I know Brock."

The cloud on my face darkened and roiled to tsunami levels. "Any friend of his is an enemy of the state. You can leave now."

"We're not…"

I cocked an eyebrow. The man had an infuriating way of almost saying something. "You have grammar Tourette's don't you?"

He chuckled. "I meant, he and I aren't friends. Brock is…" He actually blushed a little."

"There you go forking up sentence fragments again. At this rate I might get a full paragraph out of you by midnight. A page by Christmas. A book by…"

"Okay, I get it. Brock is my cousin."

"Well, I'm sorry. We can't pick our family."

He sighed. "Truth."

We stood there for a moment while he appeared to think we'd had a moment. I wasn't sure what we'd had.

"Look, whatever your name is…"

"Deggart Kincaide. My friends call me Deg."

I gave him an assessing look just to make him uncomfortable. It was a flaw I had. When faced with someone who thought he might want to be my master, I showed him my hard ass b-eye-itch to convince him otherwise. The tendency might actually have something to do with the fact that at the ripe old age of twenty-nine I was already a crazy cat lady with split ends.

Unfortunately for me, my assessing look seriously backfired. My victim was six feet two inches of deliciousness, with dark brown hair that fell across his forehead in a messy fringe, wide, full lips and dark silver eyes.

I knew I was in trouble when I started to pant a little.

"LA?"

I frowned, slapping the hand away that had been waving in front of my face. "How do you know my name?"

"Brock?"

Argh! I was going to reduce that demon to fur and nails the next time I saw him.

"Well, it's been…erm…nice to meet you, Deggart, but I'm really busy."

I grabbed the edge of the door and proceeded to shove it against him, trying to get him to leave. Turns out a door won't close over a hundred and eighty pound man.

"That's actually why I'm here. I want to help you find them."

It appeared the demon had been very talkative. "Thank you, Deggart…"

"Please. Call me Deg. Save me from my mother's ill conceived idea of a name."

I twisted my lips to hide a grin. "Deg. Thanks for the offer. But I got this."

"I've heard about your special skill."

Biting back a hiss, I fought for a conversational tone. Though it was really hard to speak through gritted teeth. "My special skill?" If Brock had told him things he had no right telling him...

"This place. It's a sanctuary, isn't it? I commend you for your work. It's about time somebody did it."

I stared at him, trying to decide if he was yanking my chain. "Um."

"Really. I spoke to an elderly calico yesterday..."

Yeah, those weren't words you heard often. "You spoke to a cat?"

"I did." He smiled. "We all have our special skills."

I frowned. "So you just, what? Meow and hiss at them and stuff?"

He grinned and my stomach went, kerplunk. "It's better than licking my butt to put them at ease."

I snorted.

His smile slipped away and he took a step closer.

I stood my ground, not wanting to show any weakness.

"They're scared, LA. Someone is hunting them. And those are the lucky ones. There've been whispers about being imprisoned in a cold, damp place."

All pretense of independence and not caring slid away as his words clanged through me like a bell. "Yeah. I've felt it." And in that moment I knew I had. It was what had been making me jumpy, taking away my sunshine for days.

"You felt what?"

Lost in a feeling I couldn't describe, I merely shook my head. "I'm sorry. I know you want to help. I appreciate that, really I do. But this is tricky and I work alone." I indicated the door and he gave me a final, long look. Finally, he nodded. "All right. But if you need me." He extended a hand and a white card slipped from between his fingers.

I blinked in surprise. I hadn't even felt a surge of energy.

"Call me. Any time of the day or night. And if you need someone to ask around…" He held my gaze for a moment, his sexy silver gaze narrowing. Then he shook his head and abruptly left, as if he'd just that moment lost all hope of making me see reason.

I kind of knew how he felt.

THE AFTERNOON PASSED SLOWLY. I went about my chores at half speed, my mind filled with dread. Every time I thought about what I needed to do my heart would start to flutter, my stomach to twist.

The cats in my sanctuary seemed to sense the turmoil in my system because they stayed away from me, perching in the very top of the trees I'd magicked for them. I had a few residents that were distrustful to begin with, and a few more that needed medical care on a daily basis. Unfortunately, short of tackling them to the ground or using my power to lure them out, I was unable to give them what they required.

I'd need to put my own house in order before my skittish friends would let me tend to theirs.

Sighing, I dropped my butt onto a rock in the grassy center of the space. A tiny meow sounded behind me and I turned to find one of three kittens I'd rescued the week before rubbing against the rock and narrowing her bright green eyes at me.

"Hey Mabel." I reached down and scooped the under-sized critter into my hand. Her tummy rumbled happily and she rubbed her face against my chin as I kissed the velvety top of her head. "At least you still love me, huh?"

The kitten was solid black, except for three white rings on her tail, and she had the greenest eyes I'd ever seen. She and her two brothers had been in an alley, cold and starving when I'd found them. I'd looked but found no sign of their mother, which was good and bad news. At least I hadn't found her dead.

The kitten curled up in my lap and gave a big sigh. I bent forward, enjoying her tiny weight and the sweet smell of her fur. Mabel ignored me for a moment, bathing her paws with a diligence that only a cat could show, then looked up and meowed softly in greeting. She rolled over onto her back and batted at a strand of my hair as I shook my head to entice her.

We played for a few minutes and, by the time the kitten jumped to the ground and ran to join her brothers beneath a weeping willow, I realized I felt better.

There was no magic in the world stronger than kitten magic. Except maybe puppy magic. I grinned at the thought and stood, determined to start the process of tracking my prey. "I'll see you all later," I announced to the standoffish crowd of felines. As I left the sanctuary, I felt a dozen pairs of eyes following me, speculation thick on the air as they tried to figure out what I was up to.

I closed the door behind me and headed down the hall toward the kitchen. It wasn't an accident that my house guests didn't know that side of my life. Hardly anybody did. In fact, I'd so far managed to keep the secret tucked tightly within my family. Others, like Brock, suspected my special abilities, but nobody knew the details of it. That was by design. I might have been born with my ability but I'd never embraced it. Even as a small child, when I'd used it to find missing pets or even, as a shy ten year old, to locate one of my friends who'd been abducted, I'd known my talent would one day get me into serious trouble. It was dangerous tracking evil. The skill put me smack dab in the cross hairs of the worst of the worst in both the magic and human worlds. Especially since I'd refused to align myself with a Witch.

I shook my head and grabbed the teapot off the stove. Filling the ancient copper pot with water, I settled it onto my antique stove and opened the oven door, wiggling my fingers until the logs inside flared into flame.

I left the water to heat and headed to my herb cabinet to gather my ingredients. A potent mixture of Eyebright, Bilberry, and Star Anise to open my higher mind. Periwinkle and Ginseng to improve cognitive function. I added a pinch of each to a tea steeper and dropped it into my favorite mug, which read "I know I look Familiar...I just have one of those faces."

The mug always made me smile.

The teapot started to sing. I grabbed my mug and turned just as a frigid blast of air swept past. I sucked air and stilled, the mug crashing to the floor and shattering.

A rotting stench rose up on the breeze, sifting foulness through my hair.

The teapot screamed into the room and evil caressed me. I fought the urge to run, knowing I could never outrun it. Instead I closed my eyes and reached for my power, feeling it already surging toward the surface of my skin. When I grabbed the hungry threads it burst, flashing like fire into the air.

My energy met the evil force and, for the briefest flare of time, I thought I could extinguish the assault. But the force invading my home was strong and savvy. It easily beat back my power. The horrible stench of brutal death assailed my nostrils, making me want to retch. I lifted a hand and began weaving magic on the air before my face, buying myself some space as the soothing scent of lavender infused my air.

The wind roared past, shoving my hair around my head so violently it hurt when it whipped against my skin. The floor beneath my feet trembled. Dishes fell from open shelves. My spell jars vibrated against the counter, some of them rattling right off to burst into shards against the floor.

I gritted my teeth and held onto my power, coating myself with it like an energy binkie as the evil force inside my home railed against me.

The energy was more than evil. It was angry. As if it knew what I was planning to do.

A renewed gust sent me stumbling back. I lifted off the ground and hit the front of my refrigerator, hanging there like a bug on a pin. I'd never felt anything like the force that pinned me there. I was all but helpless against it. And I knew that my feeble energy wouldn't be able to hold it off for much longer.

Once it got inside my barrier...

Something slammed in the direction of my front door and a deep voice called my name.

The energy assailing me eased a bit, seeming to redirect toward the front of the house.

"LA!" The voice was barely audible beneath the roar of the wind but I recognized it. Just as I somehow recognized the energy that surged toward me, slicing through the manic evil infusing my kitchen. I forced the fingers of one hand off the surface of the refrigerator, screaming with the effort it took to peel just that small part of myself free.

The borrowed energy fought to reach me, surging closer and carving off a chunk off the evil between us in the effort.

The invading force roared, its voice a putrid gale, and I got the sense it was coiling for a renewed attack.

But Deg had bought me time. With another scream, I yanked my arm free and grabbed for his energy, feeling it hit my system like a blast of fire. The power cut its way toward mine, heading for my magical core. I realized in a moment of sheer panic what it was going to do.

I screamed again, clamping down on the invading magic in an effort to stop it from reaching the center of my power. But it was unstoppable. The signature of Deg's power was a perfect complement to mine...a yin to my yang...and it found its way to my well of energy unerringly, cutting through me like a laser knife and hitting my power in a burst of light that stunned and blinded me.

I plunged away from the surface of the refrigerator as the room erupted in white light, the darkness driven back and away. A deep-throated scream rose in the distance.

My eyes were closed but I felt Deg go down. I felt his confusion...his fear as our energies roiled together into a single, terrifying force.

My muscles gave out and my face hit the floor, hard. I realized my eyes were open but I saw only white light, with silver swirls making the illumination come alive.

On some level I understood that the evil force was gone. But it no longer mattered. Because I had a new problem to address. And it was a life changing one.

In my panic, without even considering the consequences, I'd accepted the magical energy of a Witch I barely knew.

And somehow that energy had merged completely with mine.

CHAPTER FOUR

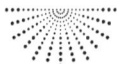

 *M*y ears were ringing. My legs and arms were too heavy to lift off the floor. And a sharp pain had moved in between my ears. The pain sliced through me in time to my heartbeat, which was much slower than it should have been…given the current circumstances.

There was a sound like somebody pounding on the bottom of a boat. For a beat I wondered if I were under-water and just hadn't realized it yet. I took a careful breath, expecting water to flood my lungs as I did. But only air slipped through my nostrils.

Along with the stench of burnt amber.

The pounding sounds started up again. I focused on the noise, felt myself frowning as my mind just couldn't identify its origin.

I needed to open my eyes and look around. But they felt as if they were glued shut.

Something moved nearby and the heartbeat in my

brain kicked up, sending shards of pain shooting through my poor skull at a rapid rate.

My hands twitched on the floor as my mind formed the thought that I should move. I was in danger and helpless on the floor.

Something touched my arm. I twitched away and forced myself to focus on the pounding, struggling to shape the noise into something I could understand. Slowly, the sound took a familiar form in my mind. The tones formed into words and my heart slowed.

I eased out a sigh as the pain slowed with it.

"LA? Talk to me, LeeAnn!"

I twitched with outrage and my lips moved without conscious thought. "Don't call me that."

A husky chuckle. "Well, at least I got you to respond." Hands smoothed over my cheek, pushing the weight of my hair away, which I realized in that moment had been splayed across my face. "Can you stand?"

I groaned softly. "I can't even open my eyes."

"I can infuse you with healing energy…"

"Don't!" I pushed against the floor, struggling against the glue holding my lids closed. Terror gave me strength and I was suddenly upright. "I've had quite enough of your magic for today."

Strong hands grasped my arms as I wobbled and I shrugged them off. I opened my eyes and focused on the man-shaped blur in front of me.

Too close. Way too damn close.

As my vision cleared I saw the hurt in his sexy silver gaze and felt a moment's guilt. "Look," I swept hair out of my face with a shaking hand and licked impossibly dry lips, "I appreciate your help. But something happened when you sent me your energy. Something I didn't like at all."

He frowned, his jaw tightening. "Yeah, sorry about that. I'd meant to give you time to adjust to the idea."

Anger pushed the last of the fog from my brain. I shoved to my feet, grabbing the edge of the counter when the world spun. "There will be no adjusting. Ever. I have no intention of tying myself to anyone. Magically or otherwise. I have my own powers. I have no desire to become someone else's sidekick."

His frown deepened. "Look, I get it…"

"Do you?" I moved away from him, bending carefully to pick up a large piece of glass. Dizziness swept through me and my mouth watered under a wave of nausea. Whatever he'd done to me had really kicked my butt. Fighting through it, I flung the glass into the trash and bent to pick up more. Tears filled my eyes as I took in the destruction in my pretty kitchen. Whatever had invaded had been the most powerful thing I'd encountered in years. Maybe ever.

"LA?"

"What!?" I spun angrily, my fists clenching. I was perfectly willing to battle for my independence. I'd always had to fight for it. I was used to combat.

Deg smiled, his eyes wary. "Do you have a broom?"

All the anger leached out of me and I deflated, feeling foolish and mean spirited. "Yeah, sorry. In the hall closet."

He nodded and turned away.

"But you don't have to help…"

"I'd like to. If you don't mind."

I watched him walk into the hallway, noting his careful movements and obvious stiffness. Clearly he was still recovering from whatever it was we'd shared. I was an ass. He'd most likely saved my life and obviously taken a physical hit as well, and all I'd done was yell at him. I dropped several more pieces of glass into the trash can, my shoes crunching on the debris spread over nearly the entire surface of my floor.

I needed to apologize for my harsh words. But I wasn't sure I could. If I was honest with myself the experience had terrified me. After all these years fighting to stay separate...apart from the world that many saw as my destiny...it might have all been wrenched away in a single, unguarded moment.

"I have one just like this."

I swung around and met his gaze, my lips curving in unspoken apology. "I suppose you use yours as transportation though."

He laughed. "Not a chance. Have you ever sat on a broom? They're dang uncomfortable."

I couldn't help grinning. "Like wearing a toothpick thong."

He laughed aloud and I felt better. The tension in the room slid away. We worked in companionable silence for a few minutes.

He emptied the dustpan into the trash and looked up. "What was that thing?"

I shrugged. "I wish I knew."

"Has it attacked you before?"

I shook my head, biting the inside of my lip as I struggled with how much I should tell him.

"Any idea why it came today?"

He was standing beside the trash can, my broom clutched in his hand, watching me with an intense gaze. I got the feeling he already knew the answer to his question. So I decided I might as well fess up. It was possible he would become a target after helping me. I wanted him to know what he was up against.

"I was prepping to do something and I think that was an attempt to stop me."

"What were you prepping to do?"

I shook my head. "That's something I'm not ready to share."

He nodded, looking down at the floor. After a moment he looked back up. "I'm sorry to pry. But can I give you a piece of advice?"

I frowned. "I guess. As long as you don't expect me to take it."

"After spending time with you today I don't have any expectations of that."

I wasn't sure if he was giving me a shot or trying to reassure me. I decided, for the sake of what might be a new friendship, to give him the benefit of the doubt. "Okay, then hit me."

"I've been a practicing Witch for a long time. I performed my first spell at five years old."

My eyebrows rose at that. "Five?"

He grinned. "I found a kitten on the street and my mom hates cats. She was allergic to them. So I magicked the cat to look like a stuffed toy whenever she was around."

I grinned. He couldn't have said anything that would have endeared him to me more. "Did it work?"

He nodded. "Until she started sneezing whenever she was around Demon. Then she wanted to throw him out and I had to fess up."

"Oh no…wait…you named a kitten Demon?"

"I did." Deg laughed. "He was pitch black with bright yellow eyes. And he was a whirlwind, always getting into things. Trust me, it was a perfect name for him."

"So what happened to Demon?"

"My aunt took him. She loved cats and she was thrilled to have him. Turned out Demon was a really good Familiar."

My smile dimmed. "Oh, he really was a demon then?"

"He was. I didn't know it at the time. I was only five after all."

Something in the way he said it made me laugh, despite the discomfort the subject gave me. "How did your mom take it?"

Deg shrugged. "She wasn't magical. She never knew about any of it. I gave my 'toy' to Aunt Maggie and she promised to keep my secret."

"You were pretty precocious as a five year old, weren't you?"

From the glint in his silver gaze I figured that five year old was still inside him. "I might have been slightly advanced for my age. Magically that is."

And devious too, I thought. But probably adorable. "I feel for your poor mother."

"Oh don't worry about her. She didn't give me the magic side, but the devious side was all her."

I burst out laughing and I suddenly realized that, despite my fear and the strange magical pull between us, I could grow to like my new neighbor. Though I had no intention of giving him any power over me.

CHAPTER FIVE

*L*ater that night, as I was mixing up a special meal for my growing kittens, the home improvement show I was watching blipped and an unwanted voice called my name. My fingers slipped on the knife I was using and I sliced a half inch cut into my finger.

"Ouch! Dangit!" I turned to glare at Brock, whose handsome face filled the TV screen. "A little warning would be nice, demon."

My first inclination that there was trouble was the fact that Brock didn't give me a cocky retort. "LA, you need to come downtown right now."

I shook my head. "I'm busy. I can't just drop…"

The picture changed to show me a tall building with a charred, smoking hole in the side, encompassing the top floors. The knife clattered to the floor, barely missing my feet, and my pulse exploded. "Tell me they're okay."

Brock came back onscreen, his sexy gaze tight with something that looked suspiciously like fear. That alone made my stomach roil. "They're…" He swallowed hard and I took a step back, as if moving farther away from the image of smoke billowing out of a gaping hole in my Grandmother's signature achievement would make the horror less real.

"We just don't know."

Blood painted crimson drops on the floor, tearing me back to reality and into action. I grabbed a paper towel, wrapping it tightly around the wound. "Nobody's been inside?"

"Yes, but they're not there."

A thin ribbon of relief swept through me. "You didn't find bodies?"

He frowned. "Not theirs, no."

His words ripped my relief away with brutal efficiency. My mother and grandmother weren't the only ones in that building. Guilt rose like bile into my throat, making it hard to breath. "How many?"

Brock just shook his head, his expression grim. "We need you here, LA. These are your people."

His words made me gasp, so close to those spoken mere hours earlier by my Grandmama. Words I'd thrown angrily back at her. My lip quivered but I resisted the pain, the fear. There was no time to be weak. "I'll be there in ten minutes."

Brock nodded and, without another word, blipped away, bringing back a pretty farmhouse with white-washed oak floors and granite countertops in a decorator kitchen. I barely noticed. I was grabbing my purse and heading out the door.

As I yanked on the driver's side door to my tiny car footsteps pounded up the sidewalk toward me. I barely glanced up. I didn't need to. I somehow knew it was him.

Deg grabbed the passenger side door and climbed into my car. The fading sun found his dark hair and painted it in gold as I slipped behind the wheel and inserted my key. The world blurred for a moment as I fought tears.

A warm hand found my thigh, squeezing gently. "We're going to find them, LA. And they're going to be fine."

I didn't question how he knew. I didn't even try to send him away. I was weak…terrified…and despite the bitter knowledge that I shouldn't need anyone else's help or support…I was extremely grateful he was there. "Thank you." I lifted my watery gaze. "Again."

He merely shrugged and turned to look out the windshield as I revved the engine and hit the gas, sending us rocketing toward the possible end of my entire world.

I wasn't sure at first what I was looking at. Or who. I flinched, realizing it would be so easy to reduce the carnage to things…to ease the horror with distance. But the outrage would give me strength. It would enhance my efforts and bring the monster who'd caused such appalling misery more quickly into my sights.

Deg was right. We were going to get him. We were going to bring my mother and grandmamma home. And what I was looking at was never going to happen again.

"…gone. Just a cosmic flare in energy and then nothing."

I turned to find Brock and Deg standing near the door, away from the gaping, charred hole in the outside wall and the super-heated air blasting through it. A soft hand touched my arm and I looked into the pretty face of Celeste's assistant. She frowned, tucking a strand of gold hair behind one ear. "I'm so sorry, LA."

I shook my head, thinking she referred to the loss of Jacob Withers, whose tattered corpse lay at my feet. "He was a good man," I said automatically. And though he'd driven me absolutely crazy at times, I knew it was true.

The woman blinked and I realized she'd been talking about my missing family. It made me angry. "All of these people," I said, swinging a hand around the devastated office where Celeste had apparently been holding a staff meeting when whatever it was hit. "They're *all* important. We need to avenge *all* of them."

The woman's face grew taut, her lips compressing, and she stepped back, away from me. Her gaze scanned toward Jacob, brows lowering in thought.

I realized I'd spoken harshly and clamped my lips closed. "I'm sorry."

She shook her head. "It's okay, dear. I understand. This has hit us all hard." Despite her words, her tone had turned cool.

"LA?"

I kept my gaze on Jacob, trying to see past the gore to the man I'd known. Deg stopped beside me, nodding toward the receptionist, whose name I'd never bothered to learn. I frowned on the thought. Why had she been spared?

"LA, we need to form a plan."

Yes. We did. "I'm going to get this bastard," I told him. "That's my plan."

"Considering this," Brock joined us and nodded toward the massive hole in the wall, "and what Deg just told me happened at your place today, I think we need a few more details in our plan."

I shook my head, frowning.

"You can't do this alone, LA," the demon said.

I clenched my hands, wondering whether it would make me feel better to punch his too-pretty face.

"LA?" Deg's soft reprimand eased past the rage and I sighed, nodding. "Okay. So let's plan. I'd like to suggest that the first step in the plan is to get this bastard."

Deg smiled. "Noted. A good step. But not a first step."

"We need to figure out who's behind the explosion and why," Brock said.

My head snapped up and I glared at him. "Who? It's the person who's been kidnapping Familiars," I barked.

Deg shushed me as several curious gazes slid our way. "LA, we need to keep that quiet."

"We don't need a full scale panic right now," the demon agreed.

I sighed, scrubbing a hand over my face. They were right. As much as I hated to admit it. I wasn't thinking straight and it was going to get someone else killed if I didn't pull myself together. I spoke more softly. "Okay. So obviously I need to track this guy."

Deg shook his head. "And suffer a repeat of this morning? I don't think so."

"It's the only way," I argued.

Brock nodded. "You're both right. LA does need to track him. But she can't do it alone. With an entity this powerful, we need safeguards and we need to proceed very cautiously."

I nodded in agreement. Deg didn't look happy but he finally nodded too. "Agreed. With emphasis on the safeguards." He shook his head. "You have no idea what we're up against, Brock. This...thing...whatever it is, blew right through LA and me. We were lucky to survive the attack."

"And that was just because I started my preparations," I said softly. "I hadn't even begun to track it yet."

Staring at the gaping hole, Brock looked thoughtful. "We might need some additional help."

"What did you have in mind?" I asked.

Deg's gaze found his cousin's and widened. "Oh no."

Brock grinned. "It's the only way, cuz."

"There has to be another way," Deg said, still shaking his head.

"If you can come up with something I'm all ears."

I was growing intrigued, despite my numb horror. "Is somebody going to tell me what you're talking about?"

Brock's grin widened. Deg looked like he wanted to melt into the floor. "It's not a what, it's a who. I think."

"No," Deg said, "it's a catastrophe."

"Tell me," I urged, losing patience.

Deg sighed. "He's talking about using a tracking expert."

Despite a quick surge of anger that they thought my abilities wouldn't be enough, I realized that, given the circumstances, another set of skills might be useful. "Why is that bad?" I asked, frowning.

"Because it's Deg's girlfriend," Brock said on a husky chuckle.

"Ex," Deg said, skimming me a quick look. "Very ex."

The girlfriend thing didn't take me to my happy place. In fact, it plunged me into a considerably darker place than I already inhabited...which was really saying something.

I didn't like the implications of that feeling. But I was determined not to explore it too closely. I forced myself to shrug. "If she can help us beat this monster I'm certainly willing to listen to her."

Deg winced. "That's good, because Mandy requires everyone to not only listen but to obey."

"Oh come on, cuz," Brock said, grinning, "she's not that bad."

"No," he said, looking about half angry. "She's worse. I'm downplaying it."

"Do you want to contact her or do you want me to do it?"

Deg expelled a frustrated breath. "I'll do it. If I don't she'll think I'm pulling a fast one on her."

"It could take a while," Brock told them. "She's been overseas on a special mission for a few weeks."

"It will take a week for her to cross the ocean on her broom," I said with what I hoped was a neutral tone of voice. Brock snorted out a laugh. "Don't get all catty on us, beautiful. If this is going to work we'll need to work together."

"Trust me," Deg said on a frown. "LA isn't going to be the problem in that area."

"If she can't join us right away we already have a problem," I told the two men. "I'm not going to sit on my hands while my mother and grandmother are missing."

"You don't have to," Deg said. "You shouldn't try to track the evil force we encountered this morning, but I don't see any reason you can't try to track one of its victims."

Hope surged. "I can put feelers out for my mother or Celeste..."

"No," Brock said. "Someone less powerful. Whatever or whoever this is, getting hold of your family is a real coup. He'll be monitoring them closely."

That made my pulse pick up. If someone was looking to grab members of my family, I wondered if I was a target too. Then I realized that morning's attack proved I was. "Wait a minute." I looked at Deg. "We assumed this morning's attack was a response to my preparations for tracking the entity. What if it was totally unrelated?"

Deg's expression told me he'd already considered that possibility. "I'm afraid we have to assume it was." He looked at Brock. "Which means she doesn't try to track anyone without my help."

"Hey!" I glowered at him. "You can just step back right now, mister. I don't work for you and I don't take orders from you or anyone."

Anger flashed briefly through Deg's gaze before he inclined his head. "Sorry. That came out wrong. Believe me that my insistence comes from a place of concern for your safety. That's it. I'm asking that you allow me to be part of your tracking efforts. I really think you're in danger, LA."

I crossed my arms over my chest, trying to smooth the frown from my face. When he put it so reasonably I could hardly refuse. Not without seeming like a total Bee-eye-itch. So I shrugged. "I wouldn't mind a little unobtrusive backup. But that means you let me do my work without interference."

He lifted his hands. "You have my word. I'll be there if you need me and other than that you won't even know I'm there."

I looked into his sexy dark silver gaze and knew he was wrong.

There was just no way I'd ever miss his presence in my general vicinity.

Not an angel's chance in Hades.

CHAPTER SIX

*D*espite what I'd said to Brock and Deg, I fully intended to try one thing alone. It was my most basic of skills, but one that sometimes achieved the best results. And I didn't share it with anyone. Not even family.

Some things were too personal to share.

Even with those you loved.

Deg closed my car door for me and leaned on the window frame. "I'll be over in an hour?"

I shook my head. "Make it two hours. I have something I need to do first."

He narrowed his gaze at me, his sexy lips tightening. I shook my head, cutting off any argument he might decide to make. "This isn't up for discussion."

He shook his head and backed away, shoving his hands into his pockets. I felt his assessing gaze on me as I started the car and backed out of my spot. I could still feel it as I pulled out of the lot and drove away, passing a long line of fire trucks as I left.

The council must have decided to allow the human emergency folks in on the fire. Or the lack of a web took the decision out of their hands. Generally the magical community chose to block our issues from the non-magic crowd, preferring to handle our problems ourselves. But without a web of magic to buffer the *Familiar, Inc.* building from humans, we apparently had no control over human intervention.

And it was that reality that worried me the most. Our ability to survive unimpeded in the human world was tied to the web. The loss of that cooperative link could endanger all of us. We needed to figure out what had happened and fix the breach. I knew the answer was connected to the abductions of the Familiars...including my family. And it seemed it would be up to me and a few others to get our people back.

Unbidden, that morning's terrifying event came roaring back to me. I shivered against the memory. I'd never felt so helpless, or been as frightened as I'd been that morning. If Deg hadn't shown up when he had...

I shook off the thought. That way lay trouble. I would have found a way to get away. I always had. There was no reason to suspect I wouldn't have prevailed again.

Except for the fact that I'd been fighting a power multiples of ten times stronger than any I'd ever encountered. And that wasn't the worst of it. The energy itself was unlike anything I'd encountered. We were dealing with something new. Something we had no experience defeating. It had no discernible signature, or a thousand signatures, depending on how you looked at it. When I'd tried to grasp a thread and tug, attempting to identify the source of the devastating force, I'd sensed more than one signature trapped within the power.

An impossibility.

I drove beneath the metal and stone entrance for *Illusory Park* and wound my way past a grassy area surrounding a sparkling pond with a unicorn fountain at its center. A small group of *Illusion City* residents lounged near the pond on folding chairs and blankets. A man and a small boy guided remote control boats across the pond's silvery surface.

The happy normalcy of the scene made what I was dealing with seem even worse. If we didn't get a handle on what was happening in the magical world, it was a real possibility that it could bleed into the non-magic world. And the thought of something that powerful stalking helpless humans struck terror in my heart.

I kept driving as the road disappeared beneath rows of overarching trees, the trunks thick with age and the gnarled branches forming an almost impenetrable umbrella over the asphalt ribbon of road.

Passing a large sign declaring the road a dead end, I kept driving. A wide wall of rock centered by a roaring waterfall appeared a half mile ahead. The intimidating wall loomed higher as I barreled toward it. Glancing into my rearview mirror, I made sure there was no one following as I hit the gas and sent my little sports car at a speedy trajectory directly toward the craggy rock face.

The wall loomed. The waterfall rushed and roared, sending a heated mist up from the pool at its base. The vapor settled over me, turned the surface of my car shiny, and made the wide, green leaves encroaching on the path-like road spray as I stormed past.

A foot away from the wall, just as my front bumper appeared ready to crash into the intimidating rock, I hit an electrical barrier, feeling the magical strands of the warding snap like a spider web over my face and shoulders. The wall disappeared, the powerful magic of the ward leaving a phantom mist behind on my damp skin and car.

The asphalt turned to gravel and then to dirt and finally, as my tires went silent over a thick layer of natural mulch, I slowed to a stop and turned off the engine.

The forest around me was thick with silence.

Though it appeared devoid of animal life, I knew that was an illusion--like everything else about the place. The woodland was the core of *Illusion City*...the pulsing heart of the city and the center of everything magical. The primordial forest was the very epitome of magic, the convergence of all magic types, earth, fire, wind and water magic, threaded together with a thin strand of dark magic to make it completely impermeable to attack.

But it was the forest's other quality I hoped to use in that moment. The place was also a portal, providing a direct path to every section of the city and the surrounding areas. It served as a multi-layered shortcut if one needed to search a large area very quickly.

But more importantly it was also a barrier...dispersing the signature and trail of magic so that it was impossible to follow. I'd found that particular quality very handy in the past, and I was hoping to make use of it again. When I attempted to track the entity at the crux of our current problem, I wanted to make sure it couldn't track me back.

I climbed out of my car and stood for a moment, sensing the area for any other auras. I felt something in the distance, but it was far enough away that I wasn't concerned. It wasn't unusual to find another magic user in the forest when I was there. In fact it would have been strange if I hadn't. I just wanted to be sure he or she was far enough away that my work would be undisturbed.

Satisfied it was safe, I quickly stripped, folding my clothes and piling them on the front seat of my car. Then I closed the door and padded into the trees. I stopped and crouched at the base of a thick-limbed Alder tree. The tree's magical properties would protect and conceal me. The Alder tree heavily favored Air magic, providing, among other things, a deep connection with the other-world, invisibility and concealment, as well as protection.

I envisioned the world from a different perspective, one in which my vision and scent capabilities were changed and strengthened. The physical changes were softened by the Alder's healing properties. Delicately sharp fangs dropped into my mouth, claws burst from my fingertips, and my body twisted under the grueling reformation necessary to complete my change. I dropped forward onto delicate white paws, the earth warm and soft beneath my pads. Thick, white fur sprang from my skin in soft, rolling waves.

The world exploded into sound. Bugs sang high above my head, their wings rasping softly on the air. Beneath the ground small, burrowing creatures sifted happily through the rich loam, and under my paws the fertile black earth softened the culmination of my change.

I stood for a moment, stretching my long body languorously, and reveled in the feeling of being a cat. The greenery beneath the Alder rustled softly and my whiskers twitched with interest. My pink nostrils flared, gauging the identity of the creature moving toward me. A recognizable scent made my mouth water, and my human brain immediately recoiled.

But not as much as the tiny, gray mouse that popped, unsuspecting from the weeds. It went completely still, black button eyes bulging in my direction and whiskers vibrating on the air.

I felt sorry for the little creature, knowing just my presence there was causing it pain, but there was nothing I could do about it, except go on about my business.

With a quick twitch of my long tail, I turned away and headed toward the edge of the forest. I could feel the magic trembling there, a gentle hum that sang through my body with every step I took. It was both a compelling and repelling energy, meant to keep all but the most diligent magic users from its use. I understood the resistance. Every use of magic had a price that must be paid. It was one of the reasons I resisted using mine. But if ever there was a time my gift was needed it was that moment. When so many innocent Familiars had become targets.

I pushed through the underbrush, sending out repelling magics of my own to keep small predators like fleas and ticks away from my shiny coat. Just the thought made my lip curl over a fang. For me, nature was as alarming as it was pleasant. A decidedly un-cat-like opinion. But I was okay with that. Unlike some of my people, I held my human side uppermost in my mind at all times. The most terrifying thing I could experience would be to fall victim to the feline part of my makeup. I'd lose the most important parts of myself if that happened.

The thought gave me nightmares.

A barrier of silvery strands thrummed on the path

ahead. Beyond the strands the forest disappeared and *Illusory Park* spread out before me. I stopped, considering if the park was the right place to start. I decided I'd rather begin in the city. And the best spot to start was *Gattler's Antiques*. The small, family run business where Brock's cousin, Tabitha was last seen.

So I envisioned the storefront and, when it replaced the park beyond the barrier, I stepped into the magic.

The spicy scent of Italian food hit me right between the eyes. My stomach rumbled hungrily as I cast a longing gaze toward the popular hole in the wall restaurant next to *Gattler's*. Giovanni's was a tiny, almost tacky spot with the best food in the city.

In my humble opinion.

Their fried ravioli was to die for.

A throaty yowl brought me out of my musings and my head snapped up to peruse the alley in front of me. A round faced, one-eyed tabby cat strolled out of the darkness, his uncut musk an invisible cloud that stained the air around me. He whipped a crooked tail arrogantly and stopped a few feet away, dropping to his muscular haunches and fixing his single, yellow eye on me. *Hey, Sugar. What's a pretty little uptown thing like you doing in my downtown world?*

I really wished I could roll my eyes. Apparently bad pickup lines didn't get any better in the feline world. Sticking my pink nose into the air, I waved my tail lazily behind me, giving him my best 'disinterested' look.

The tom cat jerked his head. *Want to go someplace and mate?*

Apparently I needed to work on my projection of

indifference. *Not even a little bit. I was wondering if you could answer some questions for me.*

He narrowed his one good eye. *And why would I want to do that?*

I started to shrug and then realized it wasn't going to work in my current form. *Because there's something stalking the felines in this city and helping me might save lives.* I deliberately left out that the lives we'd be saving weren't strictly feline. Most were human Familiars, unable to shift. Contrary to human fantasy fare, true Familiars weren't generally shapeshifters. Although about twenty percent of us were. And the ones who shifted came in a wide variety of forms. I even met a butterfly Familiar once.

The ratty tabby lifted a scrubby paw and ran his rough red tongue over it, trying for disinterest. Fortunately for me, he wasn't any better at pretending apathy than I was.

You don't have anyone on the streets you care about?

He gave the paw a few more licks and fixed his eye on me. *You might want to talk to Posh.*

Where would I find this Posh?

The street-worn tabby jerked his head toward *Gattler's*. *She squats there. The people seem determined to feed her.*

Can you describe her to me?

He chuckled darkly. *Trust me, you'll know her when you see her. She's kind of hard to miss.*

CHAPTER SEVEN

*T*here are challenges to moving through the streets as a cat. Especially a pure white cat with bright green eyes. I didn't exactly blend with my surroundings. And opening doors was a particular challenge. I sat on the sidewalk, looking up at the door to *Gattler's* and thinking people really shouldn't take thumbs for granted. They were very useful things. Of course I could always twitch my nose, Bewitched-like, and open it with magic. However, as I mentioned before, there's a price to be paid for every use of magic. So I restrict its use to times when I need it most.

Fortunately for me, the pair of giggling women who were too wrapped up in their conversation about a hookup the night before to notice a confused white cat on the sidewalk were going to solve my problem. As they approached, I scampered to hide behind a large planter filled with vibrant petunias, which, by the way, are a good choice for people looking for inspiration and fresh perspective.

The taller of the two women reached for the door handle and stopped. "You wouldn't believe what he said to me when we left the bar…"

I wished in that moment I had eyebrows I could lift. Nobody in the general vicinity cared to hear about her unfortunate date. Including the slightly older blonde woman accompanying her into *Gattler's*. I saw the blonde's revulsion in the quick tightening of her thin lips. "I'm so sick of bad pick-up lines," she said by way of cutting the other woman off.

I smiled inside. Smooth move.

"I know, right?" said the tall woman who had a large booger in her hook nose. Yeah, that's one disadvantage of looking up from cat level. But at least she finally opened the door and, quick as a wink, I slipped through between their feet.

"Oh!" said the blonde, lifting one foot off the floor as if I were an oversized mouse. I scurried beneath a circular rack containing sixties era clothing, my feelings slightly hurt by her reaction.

I mean, whatup? Cats are people too.

I watched the two women move more deeply into the store and then left my hiding spot to go in search of the apparently infamous Posh. I didn't have any luck and was eyeing a closed door at the back of the store, wondering if she was behind it, when a deep, gravelly voice accosted me.

Ya lookin' for me, cher?

I didn't *totally* embarrass myself. True, I might have given a little yowl of surprise at the close proximity of the unexpected voice, but I managed to spin around quite gracefully. Even if my tail did whip the air with adrenaline fueled exuberance. I blinked up at the creature draped, or maybe flowing, over the window seat at the front of the store.

The tabby in the alley had been right. Posh was hard to miss. Even though I'd somehow managed to do it for my first five minutes in the store.

So much for my tracking abilities.

Are you Posh?

Dat's me. The feline inclined her massive head, approximately the width of my backside. She blinked eyes that were two colors. Her left one was a blue so bright it looked unreal, and her right one was an almost iridescent gold. *Who's askin'?*

I… Stepping closer, I wondered if Posh didn't have some Cheetah in her. I'd never seen quite that coloration of black and orange spots in a domestic cat. Particularly one so fat she didn't recline so much as ooze over the seat. *I'm LA. I'm looking into Tabitha's disappearance.*

The polka-dotted feline tilted her head, narrowing her strange eyes. "'Bout time somebody came to look for dat girl."

So you noticed she was missing? I asked, jumping onto a wicker couch so we'd be at more of an equal height.

O' course I noticed, cher. Dat was some kind o' dark magic pouring through here dat day. Even ol' dead head Gattler noticed.

I swung my gaze toward the checkout counter in the far corner. The man standing behind the counter looked to be about seventy years old, with wild gray-white hair and gray and black bristles peppering his cheeks and chin. He frowned across the store at the two women, his narrow shoulders stooped with weariness. I could tell with a quick read of the auras in the store that the owner didn't have a lick of magic in him. Neither did the tall lady with the booger in her nose. Though the blonde seemed to jump a bit when I rolled my sensing magic over her, sliding a speculative blue gaze in my direction.

If I'd been human I would have frowned. Dark energy that was strong enough to touch non-magic humans was nothing to be trifled with. *Can you tell me what happened?*

Posh sighed. *I wish I could, cher. I've thought about it a hundred times since den. I was raised in the Louisiana Bayou by a voodoo Queen. I saw a lot of weird stuff in dose waterways. Strange juju and squiggy stuff dat would make your skin crawl. Dis energy had a similar feel to it. But it weren't voodoo. Dere wasn't no death magic fueling it. But it was darker than Old Mr. Gattler's thoughts anyways.*

Dark magic that wasn't fed by death... A chill swept over me. That was a new one. *What happened to Tabby?*

Posh lifted a leg as thick as my wrist and commenced to bathing, her dense black tail swinging lazily behind her.

I waited impatiently, realizing she was probably uncomfortable with the subject and wanting to give her time to adjust to it. Something told me a cooperative Posh would be a lot more productive than an uncooperative one.

The front door whooshed open and Posh's head snapped up. The strange colored eyes narrowed with speculation at the young mother clutching an untidy boy's hand. The kid caught Posh's gaze and his eyes widened slightly before his mother tugged him toward a still scowling Gattler.

"Posh?"

She was happy dat day. The big cat kept her eye on the

kid as he was pulled unwillingly across the store. He seemed to feel her perusal. His head, with its unruly cap of brown hair, swiveled continually in her direction. *Everyt'ing was normal until lunch. Dat sweet girl give me my usual bowl of tuna salad and den scratched the spots I couldn't reach jus' like I taught her.* She wriggled uncomfortably, her back leg snapping straight out behind her as she tried to make herself comfortable again. *Den a cold front moved in...*

A storm? Outside? If the entity we were looking for could manipulate weather... I trembled slightly on the thought.

Nah, not outside. Dat wind were only inside dis store. It near froze my tuna in the bowl, cher. I ain't lyin'.

Spectral influence? I asked.

She hissed a negative response. *I felt ghosts before, cher. Da Bayou be thick wid 'em. Dis no ghost. It were magic. Ugly, fractured magic. And it wrapped around dat girl like a blanket, quick as a wink. She didn't have no time to resist.*

I thought about the force that had invaded my home that morning and shivered again. Her description sounded like my own experience. *What happened then?*

Posh shook her head, an action so human it gave me pause. I realized in that moment that, whatever Posh was, she wasn't strictly feline. I considered sliding my sensing power over her but she hissed again. *Don't even think about it, cher.*

I don't know what you're talking about.

Mm hmm.

Tell me what happened next.

Dat girl went all still, her eyes glazed over, and she stumbled forward, real jerky like. It was like watchin' a zombie on TV.

I must have given some indication of my surprise

because Posh's whiskers twitched with amusement. *Don't go thinkin' I can't watch dat TV show, cher. I never missed a single episode. Dough I almost quit after dey killed off dat oriental guy.*

They're lucky they survived that, I agreed.

Truth, cher.

We sat in silence for a long moment. My thoughts had turned very dark. What Posh described sounded dire. What if Tabby's soul had been taken? What if the entity had killed her and left a shambling corpse behind? It sounded too strange to be true. But if it was, my world was about to get a whole lot darker.

Dat t'ing take somebody you care about, cher?

I blinked furiously as tears filled my eyes. *Yeah. My mom and grandmamma.*

Awe, cher. I'm so sorry.

Her pity burned like acid and I jerked to my feet… erm…paws. Suddenly I had to get away. *Thanks for your help.*

I jumped down, intending to hurry out of there. But I jerked to a halt in front of the door, realizing I'd have to use my magic to get out. The humans were all across the store and it didn't appear that any of them were planning on leaving anytime soon.

Unfortunately, the kid was staring right at me. If I magicked the door open he'd see.

The floor rumbled under a teeth-rattling thump and I jerked in terror, spinning around.

Posh ambled slowly in my direction, her body jiggling under the movement. *I'll get ya out, cher. Gattler listen to me.*

Thanks.

No problem. She batted at the door and gave off a yowl

so loud, the three women in the store jumped. The kid smiled widely and clapped his hands, clearly enjoying the Posh show.

Gattler turned a grumpy countenance in our direction and then, amazingly, smiled. "You need to go out, Miss Posh?" He came around the counter and hurried over, bending down to give the widely made feline a good scratch behind the ears. Her purr was loud enough to rattle the windows.

I'd ducked under an antique dresser when I saw him coming but I needn't have bothered. He clearly had eyes only for Posh.

"Here ya go, girl." Gattler twisted the knob and shoved the door wide. She gave him a wink and ambled on through, her tail whipping the air behind her massive backside.

I slipped quickly through on her heels. *Thanks so much for your help. I'm sorry you're stuck outside now.*

Oh, don't be sorry, cher. It's time for me ta make my rounds anyway. She gave me a wink that strengthened my belief she was more than what she seemed. *Y'all come back and see me again now. Y'hear?*

It was a promise I wasn't hesitant to make. I had a feeling Miss Posh and I would cross paths again. And I could honestly say I looked forward to it.

CHAPTER EIGHT

*O*ver the centuries, tens of thousands of magic users have fed energy into the barrier of the primordial forest. When injected into the barrier, magic energy is immediately absorbed and strengthens the warding that's already there.

Theoretically, it becomes one, cohesive structure, no longer tied to the individuals who helped build it. In fact, the forest tax had been an important obligation for every magic user for as long as I could remember. Even as a tiny spell buster of five I could remember sticking my finger into the boundary and injecting a few spurts of power.

To the naked eye, it seemed a wholly homogenous structure. But there's a moment...a beat in time...when crossing the power barrier into the forest, that the crosser is assailed by the chaos of the thousands of signatures forming the magic-made boundary. For the span of an eye blink, an alert user could catch glimpses of the barrier's contributors. It was a flash web of a sort. A record of donors that couldn't be controlled so it wasn't much use to anybody.

Very rarely something important flashes through the passer's system and it's impossible to ignore. That was exactly what happened to me as I left the downtown streets to return to my car in the forest.

I stepped inside and was, as usual, assailed by images, thoughts, feelings and even scents. One feeling in particular stopped me in my tracks. I stood inside the barrier, the current of energy from untold Witches, pure demons and demonic Familiars bombarding me, and tried to recapture the jolt of horrific fear I'd felt there. Someone had set a trigger within the boundary. A trigger meant specifically for me. And it had passed by so quickly I'd nearly missed it.

As it was, I wasn't certain I could do anything with it.

But I had to try.

The magic cascading over me tingled against my skin, its tentacles biting and abrading in an effort to expel me from the barrier. I braced myself against it and fought to reclaim the rapid-fire message. It was impossible.

Despair swept me as I realized someone had been very desperate. It was nearly unheard of to send a message through the barrier. Only done in the most dire of circumstances. And the messenger had to be within the forest.

In frustration, and as the biting energy doubled its efforts to propel me from its depths, I realized I might have better luck if I weren't in my animal form.

Though I had human thoughts for the most part as a cat, the feline brain did restrict me in some ways. So I closed my eyes and reached for transformative energy, feeling my flesh and bone twisting, elongating and transforming back to human. The pain was brief. My transformation blindingly quick inside the magic bubble, and almost as soon as it was complete, a single thought crashed into me, skittered across my senses, and dropped me to my knees.

Beware the web...barrier...death.

With a cry I was expelled from the barrier. I landed hard on the ground inside the warding, scraping across several feet of rocky ground before I came to a stop against a prickly bush.

My muscles throbbed. My head pounded. I lay there a moment embracing the look of horror that had flashed through my mind, trying to hold it close. Tears slipped silently down my face.

Feeling as if I'd gone twelve rounds with a fire demon from Hell, I crawled slowly to my feet and stumbled toward my car. I was infused with a depression so deep I wasn't sure I'd be able to do what needed to be done.

I'd seen her. I knew where she was. And I had to go gather her up.

Then I needed to contact poor Brock. And tell him his pretty young cousin was the latest victim of the thing we were trying to find.

TABITHA LAY on her side beneath the delicate branches of an Ash tree. Her hair was damp, her skin glistening under a sheen from the mist of the nearby waterfall. She looked peaceful lying there, her long, dark lashes forming perfect arcs against her pale cheeks. Her legs were bent at the knees, slender feet inside inexpensive flip flops. She wore fringed denim shorts that barely covered her behind and a tee shirt with a glitter-enhanced broom on the front that read, "I brake for falling stars."

The shirt made me smile, even as tears slipped down my face.

Reaching out, I pulled my courage around me and touched her cheek. I expected a single, electrical jolt, her magic recognizing mine, but got instead a flare of electricity that sent me backward with a yelp. The stench of death magic filled my sinuses and I grimaced.

The energy infusing Tabby's body wasn't her own.

The touch left an oily, cold feeling on my fingertips. It made a darker stain on my heart. Sudden, almost violent rage filled me. The person who'd killed Tabitha needed to die. He deserved only the harshest death. And I was going to make sure he got it.

I blinked, shocked by my own thoughts, and pushed to my feet. I did a quick perusal of the body, making certain I didn't touch her again, and saw that one long-fingered hand was fisted as if she were holding something. I got down on my knees, examining the hand, which was stretched high above her head and covered in defensive bruises. I couldn't see what was inside. Her fingers were clutched too tightly.

Finally, I bit down on my fear, tensing against the expectation of pain, and grasped her hand. Nothing happened. Whatever had hit me before seemed to have been a one-shot deal. I quickly pried her fingers open and jerked back, feeling shock like a punch to the gut.

The killer had carved a bloody X in her palm, the

edges torn and black as if he'd used a burning knife to create it.

Bile rose up in my throat and I surged to my feet, stumbling away from the body. I fought nausea, pacing a dozen feet away from Tabby with my hand over my mouth. I dreaded what I had to do next.

But it couldn't be helped. Still, I let myself get lost in the oblivion of movement for a few more moments, until, conscious of encroaching darkness, I knew I had to face the task.

Pulling air into my lungs, I forced one foot in front of the other and returned to Tabby.

Her glazed, brown eyes stared up at me, filled with accusation.

She'd called out to me in her moment of fear. Begged me for help.

But I hadn't heard. I hadn't known. Why hadn't I? The web had always kept us safe. In numbers we were strong. We could rely on each other for safety, for help when we needed it. But the web was down. Like Tabby, many of us had gone missing, gotten cut off from the safety of the group, our place in the connection weakened. And Tabitha had died because of it.

Shaking off the guilt, I reached out and placed my hand over her eyes, gently drawing the lids closed. Then I sat back on my heels and closed my own eyes, sending magic up my arm and into Tabitha's cold flesh.

I expected to feel a spark of life that I could grasp. It was rare for every ounce of life to leave a body upon death. Not immediately. Some small speck of magic usually remained long after, allowing me to make use of my special skill.

Finally, after searching for several moments, I felt something move deep in her core. It didn't feel like energy. It felt cold and dark, gelatinous against my spectral touch.

Revulsion swept through me at the touch and it was all I could do not to pull back from it. But I needed to find out what I could from Tabby's last moments so I gritted my teeth and held my ground. The thing inside Tabby twitched against my touch, spread slightly as if testing the energy, and then expanded with a jerk and wrapped itself tightly around my magic.

I made a helpless sound of fear, trying to pull my energy back, but it wouldn't come.

I started to panic. Cold, oily evil infused my magic and started to climb toward me. I suddenly knew that, if I didn't manage to extricate myself, it would climb all the way out of her body and into mine.

I couldn't let that happen. Panic flared, tightening my lungs until I started to hyperventilate. A figure rose up in my mind's eye. It was Tabitha, pretty and smiling. She blipped like a bad hologram and started to lift one hand in my direction. Blood ran from the corner of her mouth and her twitching and blipping became more manic, almost as if something were fighting her.

She smiled, speaking my name softly. *Let me go, LA.*

I shook my head, tears falling down my cheeks. "I can't."

You have to. Let us all go so you can find us again.

I shook my head as ice climbed up my arm. It felt as if something living moved just under my skin and I shuddered under its touch. "I don't want to lose you."

Tabby blipped again, going nearly black, and when she

eased back into view her smile was gone. She lifted her hand and showed me her palm. *It lives here, feeding where we join. It hungers...*

As she spoke the air around her blackened, obscuring and thickening until all that was left was her eyes. They pinched in pain, then widened in horror. *Let me go, LA. They're all counting on you.*

I sobbed as her entire visage disappeared, cloaked in oily, shimmery black. Its icy presence weighed down my chest and my lungs would no longer expand beneath it. I tried to take a deep breath but couldn't. For a moment I thought I'd somehow fallen into water and was drowning.

It didn't matter if that were true or not. The end result would be the same.

If I couldn't free myself from the black energy, I would die.

The ground came up to meet me and I slammed into it. My legs wouldn't move. My arms were stiff and frozen. A foul stench filled my sinuses, as if I'd fallen into a pit filled with death.

Numbness eased over me, coating the panic in thick layers of detachment. Maybe I could just rest for a while. I was suddenly so tired.

A frigid cloud enveloped me, strong winds buffeted me back and forth. The ice climbed through my body, easing down my legs. Its glacial touch slid up the back of my neck, heading toward my mind. Somehow I knew if it reached my brain I was gone.

You have to fight! An insistent, really irritating voice in my head told me.

But I was so tired. Maybe I'd just rest a minute...

No! The voice nagged.

I frowned. *Shut up annoying voice.*

LA!

I think I shook my head. I wanted to smack the owner of the voice but I wasn't masochistic enough for that.

Dammit, LA! You need to fight.

"You're very annoying," I told the voice.

"LA, let the energy go."

I blinked. Wait a minute. My voice wasn't that deep.

Frantic hands slipped down my arms, rubbing them with brusque efficiency. My teeth clanked together and I felt the cold again. "So cold," I told the voice.

"I know, honey. You need to let the energy go. As long as you fight it he'll hold on."

I shook my head, shuddering violently. "I can't let go of her. I have hold of her life force. Maybe I can pull her back."

The hands were strong but gentle as they tugged me off the ground, into a warm cave. When the voice spoke again it was in my ear. "She's gone, LA. You need to let her go."

I tried to open my eyes but my lids were frozen shut. I shook my head. "She needs me…"

"LeeAnn Mapes!"

I jerked at the booming voice and my eyes shot open. I found myself looking into Brock's angry face hovering over me. "She's gone. She doesn't need you anymore, but *we* do. Now snap out of it and let go of that thing!"

I frowned, licking my lips. "I can't believe I thought you were kind and caring."

He lifted twin, coal black eyebrows. "Demon?"

"He's right, LA, you need to let Tabby go. Now. Before the entity gets any deeper into you."

I jumped, realizing the warm cave was talking. I turned and gave Deg a smile, feeling punch drunk. "There's the kind and caring."

"Dammit, LeeAnn!"

I jumped as Brock bellowed my name, managing to lift a hand in his direction. I shot a short stream of energy into his muscular thigh and he jumped, swearing as he rubbed the spot. Just like that, the frigid cold was gone and warmth eased through my body. Especially the parts that were in contact with the yummy and sizzling hot Deg. "Has anybody ever told you, you're not very nurturing," I told a storm-faced Brock.

The warm cave laughed. "That's my girl."

Pushing against his chest, I tried to stand and my muscles screamed. I almost fell again. Deg leapt to his feet and grabbed me, pulling me close as my knees wobbled.

"Slow down. You just survived about a ninety percent magical infiltration. It's going to take a while for your body to recover."

I gently shoved him away. "I'm okay." When I turned to look at Brock, guilt burned through me like acid. I shouldn't have teased him. He'd just lost his favorite cousin.

He stood looking down at Tabby, his expression dark and his muscles taut with rage.

"I'm sorry, Brock."

His response was to stiffen more. His shoulders were rock, his jaw steel. He didn't speak.

"Let's get you home," Deg said softly.

I shook my head. "We need to take care of her."

Deg lowered his gaze to the prone Familiar and pain flashed through his dark silver eyes. In that moment I remembered he was related to Tabby too. "I'm sorry for your loss, Deg."

He nodded, his lush mouth tightening as emotion swept him. "Thanks."

"I'll take care of her," Brock told them without turning.

I hesitated, wanting to argue. He shouldn't have to deal with Tabby's death alone.

But he seemed to sense my hesitation and turned, his expression filled with rage. "Go, LA."

I let Deg lead me away then. Brock needed to do things his way. He'd always been like that. Not for the first time I thought how lonely he must be because of it.

Then I realized he wasn't all that different from me.

And the loneliness found me too.

CHAPTER NINE

I'd tried to rest but my mind wouldn't allow it. I couldn't help going over and over the short interaction with Tabitha's spirit, wondering how much of it was actually her and how much represented the poisonous entity hidden inside.

Her words confused me. Other than sounding too dramatic to fit the once fun-loving personality of the Familiar who'd spoken them, they were more dire than informative. If Tabby was trying to help me discover the person who'd killed her, why'd she give me information in soundbites from a horror movie? And what was with the X carved into her hand? Was the killer marking his conquest...á la X marks the spot of my last victim...or did it mean something else? I thought about what the symbol could mean, coming up with the Roman numeral for ten. Had he killed ten familiars already?

The thought depressed me and made me jittery with nerves. I was no closer to finding our villain than I'd been when I'd started. And it seemed that every time I attempted to forge a path to him I was attacked instead.

Each time nearly dying in the process.

I sighed, tugging a clean shirt over my wet, shoulder-length hair. My hair stuck to the soft fabric, clinging damply, and I fought the tangles to free it.

I glanced at the clock. Deg had told me he'd return around midnight. Apparently his ex-girlfriend was arriving at ten and he was going to pick her up and bring her to my house so we could confer.

I wasn't sure what the woman could do that I hadn't already tried. Though, to be fair, I'd been stopped in my tracking pursuit before I could get very far.

Maybe she'd have better luck than I in sneaking past the entity.

My doorbell rang and I frowned. Deg was over an hour early and I still needed to do a final check on my sanctuary visitors before I closed down for the night. Grabbing a nylon-bristled brush from my dresser, I headed toward the door, struggling to brush through the wet tangles of my still dripping hair as I went.

I was not feeling particularly pleased with the upcoming meeting. I had a sneaking suspicion I wasn't going to like Deg's ex any more than I suspected she'd favor me.

I opened the door with a frown on my face. "You said midnight. You're early."

The woman standing with her fist in the air, ready to pound on my door again, didn't even blink. She simply shrugged. "Actually, I didn't say any time. I just showed up. I always find that catching people off guard tells me more about their strengths and weaknesses than anything else."

I stood there with my mouth open and one hand squeezing a section of my hair with the towel.

My mute surprise didn't have any effect at all on the woman I presumed was the infamous Mandy. Deg's "very" ex girlfriend. She had coal-black hair she wore pulled straight back in a high ponytail. The hair shone in blue highlights in a non-existent light and bounced in a thick fall behind her head as she returned my perusal with one of her own. She was tallish, probably three or so inches taller than my five feet four, and her oblong face sported high cheekbones and caramel colored eyes that slanted up exotically in the corners. Her lips were lushly made, exuding sex-appeal even when pinched slightly with annoyance as they currently were.

"Are we going to just stand here all night?" she asked impatiently.

I looked around for Deg but he didn't seem to be with her. "Where's…"

She pushed past me with a smug grin and entered my house uninvited. Standing in the hallway of my elderly Victorian jewel, she put hands on hips and took it all in. "Very nice. I see you're connected with the past. There's much to be learned there." She nodded approvingly. Then, turning to me with that same smug grin, she chopped my legs off at the knees. Figuratively speaking of course. "But it also puts you hopelessly behind times on the updated magic forms."

I snapped my mouth closed and lowered the towel. As I set my jaw and pushed the door closed, I contemplated whether Deg and Brock would notice if I turned her into a toad.

Speaking of the old ways.

"If you'll just show me where you want to do this, I'll get set up," she said in her superior tone of voice.

"Do what?" I asked. Despite my best intentions, frustration threaded my tone. The woman hadn't been in my home for five seconds and I was already on my heels, out of sorts, and frustrated beyond belief.

Although to be fair, I'd been annoyed before I even met her so I couldn't completely blame her for that. But I was willing to try.

"Kitchen?" she chirped brightly. "Works for me." She turned on her heel and headed straight for my kitchen at the back of the house. I had no idea how she knew where it was.

"Hold up!" I hurried after her, reaching for her arm. I closed my hand around the slender limb and found myself clutching air. When I looked up in shock I discovered her standing a couple of feet away, the smug smile still firmly attached to her face.

I was really starting to hate the…erm…Witch starting with a B. "I don't know you and I didn't even invite you into my house." I shook my head. "You can't just barge in here, insult me, and make yourself at home in my kitchen."

She cocked her head, caramel-brown gaze sparking with humor. "Can't I?"

I expelled air, my frustration bringing magic roaring to the surface. My fingertips tingled as razor-sharp claws tried to emerge and delicate pulses, like the touch of thousands of tiny spider feet, danced over my skin. If she wasn't careful she was going to get a fistful of energy between her condescending eyes.

Amazingly, she laughed. "First, I'm not a vampire. You don't need to invite me in."

"I know that…"

"And B, I just proved I *could* do all those things so your point is moot."

Before I could stop it, my foot slammed down on the shiny hardwood floor. I might have made a small, frustrated noise too. "But it's rude."

The amusement in her gaze grew. She ignored my statement as if it didn't matter one whit. I guess it really didn't. Clearly Mandy the Witch with a B didn't care about human niceties. "And three, Deggart told me we were meeting here so, actually, I *was* invited."

I glared at her. "No, I was expecting Deg to bring you here. *He* was invited. You weren't." I knew it was a distinction without a difference but she'd really hacked me off so I wasn't going to give her an inch. "Where is he, by the way?"

She turned to the door, narrowed her gaze, and said, "Bottom of the steps. He'll be knocking just about…"

Two hard, fast knocks sounded on my door.

"Now." Mandy slid a hostile gaze over me and crossed her arms, daring me to cast her out.

I sighed, turned, and headed for the door just as it opened. Deg's face was filled with apology. "Is she here? She's here isn't she?" He came through the door, scrubbing a hand over his jaw. "I'm so sorry, LA. I should have known better than to think I could control her."

I turned as something slammed to the floor at the back of the house. Sure enough, the infuriating Mandy was no longer standing in my hallway. "She just barged in," I told Deg with disbelief in my voice.

He shook his head. "I know. I'm sorry. She thinks it's cute to do that."

"I can hear every word you're saying, you know."

I jumped at the sound of her voice right over my shoulder. But when I turned she wasn't there. In fact, I could still hear her slamming around my kitchen.

Deg rolled his eyes and nodded toward the back. "Shall we?"

I let him guide me to my kitchen hoping he'd be able to control the B-eye-Witch better than I'd been able to so far.

It wasn't a strong hope. I had a feeling Mandy whatever her last name was had been running people over her entire life.

Sure enough, by the time we entered the room, Mandy had several of my baking sheets spread out on the counter and she was covering them with an assortment of herbs. She glanced up when we walked in, giving Deg a sexy smile. "Deggart. You're looking yummy as always."

He flinched when she used his full name, his mouth tightening. I realized he'd probably asked her to use the shorter version as he'd done me, but she'd ignored his request as she probably ignored pretty much anything she didn't want to do. "Mandible. I see you're locked on and forging straight ahead as usual."

She laughed lightly at his distortion of her name but I didn't miss the annoyance flashing through her gaze. "Still prickly about the name thing, I see."

"Here's an idea," he told her through gritted teeth,

"why don't you just use the name I ask you to use? Then I won't have to be prickly."

"And you presumably would no longer be referred to as a jaw bone," I added sweetly.

She snapped an irritated glower my way but it passed so quickly from her expression I could have mistaken it. "There's power in names, Deggart. You should embrace yours. It will set you free."

"It's more satisfying just to set you free," he mumbled.

Her answering laughter lived on the air beside my ear. Her face never moved as she opened my oven and slipped the pans inside.

I'd love to know how she projected her voice like that. It seemed like it could be a handy trick.

Mandy closed the oven doors and frowned down at the controls. "How do you work this thing?"

I allowed a smug smile to cross my face as I pushed her out of the way and lit the oven.

"Wow," she said, shaking her head. "When I said you were in touch with the past I had no idea."

"The stove burns Baobab wood mixed with Ash for advanced magic, ancient awareness, divine communication and spiritual power."

Mandy frowned. "You can get the same effect by adding liquid essence."

"I don't think the essence fuses with the magic as strongly. The smoke gives it an extra zing."

Shrugging, Mandy opened the door and sent a stream of energy into the smoldering wood, bringing it back to flame. "I can see that actually. Maybe we'll do both."

I was a bit surprised she agreed with me. Clearly she was a Witch who liked more modern ways of performing magic. My methods were nearly as old as the Earth. "It can't hurt, I guess."

There was a choking sound behind us and we both turned to find Deg looking strained. He crossed his arms over his chest and glowered down at both of us. "Can we move this along, please? People are dying."

I stared at him, shocked he'd throw more pressure onto us. Then I looked deeper into his eyes and saw the pain and fear there. What I didn't know was if the fear was because of the enemy we were trying to defeat, or because his scary ex-girlfriend had inserted herself firmly into his life again. "We're moving as quickly as we can, Deg. This thing we're fighting has proven the ability to find us when we try to stop it. I thought we'd agreed to be careful."

He glanced away, a flush infusing his handsome features. "You're right. I'm sorry. I'm a little stressed about Tabby."

I touched his arm as the earthy scent of burning wood filled the kitchen.

Mandy lifted the damper on the back of the stove and placed a jar over it to gather some of the smoke. She placed the special brass lid over the jar to keep the smoke from escaping and then opened her oversized bag and perused the contents.

"We need stealth," I told her.

She nodded, reaching for a small vial filled with flat, black liquid and shaking a few drops into the jar. The contents exploded in a silver spray that dripped slowly down the inside of the jar.

"Intuition," Deg added. Mandy threw him a tight smile. "I got this, Witch."

He expelled air through his nose and leaned against the counter as Mandy selected a vial of purple dust, sifting some into the jar. The silver and purple met in a flash flame that left behind a blood red liquid which shimmered under the overhead lights.

Next she grabbed a small jar of a gray paste that she dipped her finger into and scraped off into the jar. Nothing happened but as the mix hit the shimmery ooze at the bottom it seeped slowly into it, disappearing as if it had never existed.

"What was that?" I asked, curious despite my reluctance to appear stupid.

Mandy lifted the jar and eyed the contents carefully, shaking it a bit. "It's my strengthening additive. It will enhance everything we add to the potion, doubling its power."

"You forgot Eye of Newt," Deg mumbled sourly.

I bit the inside of my lip to keep from smiling. Mandy just shook her head. "Respect, Deggart. Everyone has her own way of doing things."

"I'll take that under advisement," he told her, throwing me a look that carried meaning I couldn't decipher. "As soon as you return the favor."

She stamped her foot, turning to him so quickly the jar slipped out of her fingers. I lunged for it but it danced away from my touch, hanging on the air near Mandy's shoulder. She put hands on hips and glared at Deg. "Look, Witch, I understand your ego won't let you get over that whole gargoyle thing..."

"It's not ego, Mandy. You almost got us killed..."

"...but my methods work if you give them a chance," she continued as if he hadn't spoken.

"Except when they don't."

"I'm not your damn Familiar!" she shouted angrily. The potion jar jiggled with agitation on the air and I tried again to grab it before it shot off and smashed into the wall.

"No!" he shouted back, advancing on her. "You killed him."

I jerked back, my eyes going wide. "She what?"

Mandy threw me an impatient look. "He's being overly dramatic."

"Did you or did you not give Rick a spell for gargoyle extinguishment that failed?"

"Yes, of course I did but…"

"And did the gargoyle subsequently eat him?"

I gasped, my hand flying to cover my mouth. I took a step back as horror swept me. "Eww!"

Mandy shook her head, turning to me with an earnest expression. "It didn't happen like that, I assure you."

"As I recall, you assured Rick the potion would work too."

Mandy stamped a foot. "It *should* have worked!" Her gaze shimmered suspiciously. I looked at Deg and he must have noticed the unshed tears too. Unfortunately, his reaction to them was vastly different from mine.

"Cut the crying act, Amanda. I'm not falling for it again. And I'm not going to stand back and let you harm LA!"

That just pissed me off. "Whoa! It's not your place to protect me. I'm fully capable of protecting myself."

Deg threw up his hands and stalked out of the kitchen. I felt kind of bad for yelling at him again when he was just trying to keep me safe, but Dangit! I couldn't have him thinking he had power over me. He wasn't my Witch and I wasn't his Familiar. Despite what our magic seemed to believe. And the sooner he got that through his thick head the better.

"LA?"

I blinked, realizing Mandy had been talking to me. She held the jar again and the potion at the bottom was a glossy, silvery green. "This is ready. Are you?"

I threw a last glance toward the door Deg had disappeared through and nodded. "Yeah. I'm ready. Let's see what we can see."

CHAPTER TEN

We went into my study, which consisted of a twelve foot by twelve foot room with built in bookshelves on three walls. The fourth wall had a set of French doors leading to my small back yard. The brick patio beyond the doors was bordered in planting boxes filled with herbs and flowers for my spells. The room contained no furniture. There was only a large, handmade rug in the center with a protective circle woven into it.

Mandy smiled when she saw the rug. "Nice. I should do this at my place."

I couldn't stop a grin from forming under her approval but I quickly squelched it, chastising myself. I didn't care what any other magical being thought, I told myself. I especially shouldn't care about the opinion of an apparently dangerously cocky Witch. "Thanks. Shall we get started?"

As we sat down in the center of the circle, the door to the study drifted open and a tiny head popped through the opening near the floor. A pair of startling green eyes blinked over at us before a tiny body slipped through on a plaintive meow, short striped tail snapping. "Hey, Mabel. How'd you get out of the sanctuary?"

The kitten rubbed herself against my thigh and lifted her head so I could scratch under her chin. She narrowed her eyes as my fingernails did their magic and her purr rumbled loudly through the room.

Mandy made a small sound of pleasure and reached a finger out to scratch the tiny kitten between its velvety black ears. "She's adorable."

I smiled. "I know, right? I'm really tempted to keep her."

As if approving my suggestion, Mabel gave a happy chirp and dropped to the ground, going belly up so we could scratch her soft, round tummy.

Mandy and I both laughed, for a moment lost in the joy of petting the wriggling baby. But after a minute Mabel nipped playfully on Mandy's finger and jumped to her feet, bouncing away from us as we laughed. She jumped onto one of the lower shelves and climbed up to sit on a thick, dusty volume of transformative spells.

Which was our cue to get to work.

Mandy placed the spell jar at the center of our protective circle and looked at me. I nodded, lifting my hands and working my fingers on the air as I spoke the spell to close the circle. A beat later it snapped closed with a sizzle that brought the kitten off the shelves to sit at the edge of the rug. She cocked her head, narrowing her expressive gaze as Mandy reached out and opened the jar.

She grasped my hand and immediately began chanting her spell. The silvery green potion shimmered as if shaken and then began to climb the walls of the jar, oozing through the opening at the top and sliding down the sides. As it hit my warded rug it sizzled, turning instantly to mist. The green-tinged mist rose in a circle above the jar and spun there, gathering speed as Mandy's chanting gained momentum.

Magic filled the circle, its sulfurous scent making my nose twitch and calling to my own energy, which throbbed against my skin in time to my rising heartbeats. Mandy's fingers were cool in mine, her grip loose. She calmly built the magic within the circle, dropping her head back as it slipped over us, caressing my skin with moist, slightly clammy fingers.

The feel of her tracking magic was so very different from mine. But within its constraints I could feel the elemental building blocks of stalking energy. The energy formed a passage through the layers of time and space, like a portal that allowed us to visualize the location of the one we sought.

At first the swirling black hole that opened in the air before us hid our prey, cloaking him in a curtain of obscuring magics. I felt the strength of his warding against my skin, like a dozen bees stinging my flesh. My stomach tightened with dread, reacting to the ominous warning within the ward.

I fought the urge to slap at the biting magic, knowing it would only make it worse. Our only respite from the pain was to push forward, surging past his wards until we could see his face, read his magic signature.

The mist lightened somewhat, turning charcoal gray, and I could see movement through its opaque surface. Mandy's chanting sped even more, until her words tumbled together so quickly I couldn't tell one from the other. But I could recite the magic from memory, the Latin as well-known to me as my own mind. She squeezed my fingers and I complied, joining my voice with hers as the mist continued to swirl, lightening another shade.

The violence of the ward's reaction had become almost unbearable. It felt like razor wire digging into the surface of my skin, so violent in its purpose I thought if I looked down at my arms they'd be bleeding.

My voice grew louder as I dug deep for determination. We almost had him. We were so close. I could feel his panic in the renewed assault of his wards. But as close as we were, there was no shadow of a specific signature written in the mist. We were near enough to tracking him that I should have been able to read the mark of his magic imprint. It wasn't that I couldn't see it. The mark was there, but it was a chaos of identities, almost as if we were dealing with several people instead of just one.

The moment I had the thought the mist disappeared and I was looking at the back of someone's head. The focus was tight, too tight to tell if it was a man or a woman. I had the sense it was a man, but as the figure turned, wide blue eyes fixing on me with a deadly glint, I felt their evil power like a punch to the gut.

And something about them was uncomfortably recognizable.

Beside me Mandy's chanting faltered. Her fingers tightened on mine and I felt her stiffen as the hard, blue gaze turned to her and widened slightly.

A slender blonde eyebrow lifted in silent question and Mandy jerked her hand from mine just as a surge of deadly energy shot from the portal. "Get out!" Mandy shrieked, the energy spearing into her chest, right where her heart would be.

She stood jerking, her eyes wide and filled with terror and her limbs flopping as the magic threw her around like a rag doll.

I screamed her name, knowing I had to do something to help. But I couldn't think of a thing to do, other than step in front of the energy myself. I was moving forward to do exactly that when a yowl filled the air.

I spun as a small, midnight form shot off the ground and flung itself at the portal. The tracking gateway exploded outward with a shriek and then collapsed upon itself, closing to a pinprick on the air and then snapping off with a whine.

Mabel's tiny form dropped to the rug and lay unmoving.

I realized as I threw myself at Mandy, that the tiny kitten had probably saved both our lives. Unfortunately, I was terrified she'd done it at the expense of her own.

CHAPTER ELEVEN

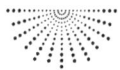

*T*he door to the study slammed open and Deg called my name. I looked up and my expression must have been as horrified as I felt. He hurried over. "What happened?"

"He hit her in the heart with a major power blade. She's not breathing."

Deg looked angry. "You contacted him without me?"

I huffed out a breath. "This is not the time. We need to help her."

Deg shook his head. "We'll discuss this later."

"Whatever." I placed my hand over her face and closed my eyes, beginning a chant to locate Mandy's life force. If I could find a spark maybe we could help it grow and strengthen. Deg moved closer and started a chant of his own. It wasn't Latin and I couldn't follow it entirely but I did catch a couple of the words from the Demonic Script and it made my heart race. Was he using black magic?

I opened my eyes to ask and gasped. Deg sat cross-legged beside Mandy, one hand on the warded rug and the other flat against her chest, just above her breasts. An orange light pulsed from the hand touching Mandy and his shoulders drooped, fresh lines of weariness etching his handsome face.

I watched in amazement as Mandy's chest began to rise and fall, her eyelids fluttering softly.

When I was sure she was going to pull through, I touched him on the shoulder and gave him a little shake. "Deg, it's okay now. You need to stop."

His head was lowered nearly to his chest and his color wasn't good. It too closely resembled the pale gray ash we'd seen at the *Familiar, Inc.* fire. Still, he didn't stop. His color faded to white and his mouth was pinched, lips cracked and bleeding.

I tried to pull his hand away from Mandy and received a major shock that speared through me, sending me scuttling backward on a yelp. "Deg, stop it, now!"

He jerked and sucked air, closing his hand to extinguish the energy. But when he opened his eyes the whites were crimson with broken blood vessels. He sat back, scrubbing a badly shaking hand over his jaw.

"Oh my god! What did you do to yourself?"

He shook his head. "I'm fine."

"You're not fine. You look like somebody sucked half the life right out of you."

His cracked lips firmed and he shoved slowly to his feet, his broad back curved with weariness.

Mandy began to stir almost immediately. Her eyes blinked open and she tried to sit up. "What happened? I feel like I've been hit by a truck."

"You were zapped by an energy arrow as thick as my

arm," I told her, eyeing Deg worriedly. "Deg, are you sure you're okay? You don't look good."

Mandy took one look at him and frowned. "Deggart, what did you do?"

His smile was grim. "Something I probably shouldn't have."

She stiffened. "You shared your life force with me, didn't you?"

My mouth fell open. "Is that even possible?"

Mandy groaned, holding her head as if the room were spinning.

It was a stupid question, not worthy of an answer. Mandy had been a breath away from dead and Deg had brought her back to life.

"I didn't do it just for you," he said softly.

I reached out as he swayed, nearly hitting the rug face first. "You should lie down."

He nodded. "Just for a minute."

I helped him lie back on the rug and he sighed, patting my knee with a still shaking hand. "Thanks."

"Don't thank me, tell me what you did. Why did you ground yourself in the protective circle?"

He blinked in surprise. "You noticed that, huh?" He actually smiled. "Good work."

Though the smile transformed him, making him look a bit more like the wickedly handsome Witch he'd been before draining himself nearly dry, I frowned, offended by his praise. "Let's cut the condescension shall we?"

His smile disappeared. "I didn't mean…"

"Forget it." I didn't want to hear excuses. I wanted explanations. "Just tell me what you did."

He took a deep, shaky breath. "What I'd intended to do

all along, except that I had to infuse the magic with healing properties too." He threw Mandy an accusatory look. Clearly he blamed her for our little foray into unsanctioned tracking. I'd have to set him straight. Later. After he explained what he was about.

"I simulated the signature of the power he sent into Mandy. Then I infused the protective circle with it so it would have built in warding when we tried to read it."

I frowned. "I tried to scan that energy. It was a chaotic mess."

Mandy nodded, finally pushing to her feet. She stopped, wobbling slightly and bent forward, hands on knees. "I did too. If I didn't know better I'd think it was a dozen people combining energy."

"That's exactly what it is," Deg said, his sexy mouth set in a grim line.

"But that's not possible," I told him. "Besides, we saw the culprit. It was one person."

Deg's eyes went wide. "You saw him?"

Mandy and I shared a look. My pulse picked up at the memory of those hate-filled eyes. "Actually, it was just his eyes."

"And a fringe of light-colored hair," Mandy added.

Deg's color was returning and he seemed more comfortable. When he sat up he no longer looked like he was going to fall over. He frowned, resting his forearms on his knees. "Somehow then, one person is channeling the power of several magic users."

"That's never been accomplished before," Mandy said, looking doubtful.

"I think we can safely say this guy, whoever or whatever he is, isn't our usual magic user."

"True," she admitted.

Then I remembered what Tabitha's soul form had told me. I looked at Deg. "That makes sense."

"What makes sense?" he asked, frowning.

"What Tabby told me when I read her residual life force."

He looked surprised but nodded for me to continue.

"Her message was impossibly cryptic, but she mentioned the web and the barrier."

To Deg's credit he caught on quickly. "Both sources of collective magics."

"Yes."

We stared at each other a beat, sharing the moment of revelation and, in my case at least, considering potential consequences.

Mandy cleared her throat, drawing our attention back to her. "Don't forget the shared web is dead. Right now the magic community is blind to what everyone is doing."

I realized in that moment what she was telling me. Shock made the room spin. My heart pounded and my knees weakened. I lowered myself to the rug before I fell. One hand slid down to caress the soft strands that hummed slightly from the infused magic. "Gods." The implications were terrifying. "So he's taken the web."

"Which means he's the only one who knows where everyone is…" Mandy said.

"And what we're doing," Deg nodded.

"Talk about your tracking devices," I whispered as my belly churned with dread.

"It gets worse," Deg said, frowning. "If my speculation is right, this guy didn't just steal the web. He *is* the web."

Mandy gave a soft intake of air and I stared at Deg, my shock too great for words.

We sat mute for a long moment. The stunned silence was finally broken by an unexpected and very welcome sound.

CHAPTER TWELVE

*M*eow!

My gaze jerked downward as a soft body rubbed warmly against my leg. *Mabel!* I'd momentarily forgotten about the tiny kitten. With a happy exclamation I bent down and scooped her up, getting a contented rub against my chin for the effort.

I held the kitten close, laughing as her purr rumbled loudly through the room.

"Is she okay?"

I turned to Mandy, grinning widely. "She seems to be fine."

Mandy was frowning, looking perplexed. "But she..."

I shook my head, squeezing the tiny critter tightly enough to elicit an alarmed yelp. "Sorry, baby girl," I murmured as I forced my grip to loosen. "I just can't believe you survived. That was a very brave thing you did."

Mandy's frown deepened. Why didn't she look happier? "What's wrong?"

Her gaze found mine and it was filled with worry. "There's no way that kitten should have lived through a jolt of energy that big. It almost killed me."

"Tell me what happened," Deg demanded, earning himself a glower from me and his former girlfriend. "Just tell me. Please?"

"He was killing her..." I said quietly, suffering a flash of guilt that I hadn't been able to stop it. I shook my head. "I don't know how...or why...but one minute Mabel was on the book shelves and the next..." I frowned at the memory. It didn't seem possible the kitten could have known how to stop the assault. Could she have simply reacted to an invading energy?

"She threw herself at the portal," Mandy said. Her frown had smoothed away and she was staring at the kitten with a look of awe.

"There's no way she was trying to get to you?" Deg asked me.

I shook my head. "I was a couple of feet away. No. She leapt directly at the portal."

Deg swung his gaze toward the kitten. "Then what happened?"

I shrugged. "The energy hit her and stopped."

"Stopped?" he asked, looking dubious.

"Actually," Mandy said. "It appeared to repel, curling back on itself. And then the portal snapped shut."

We all stared at Mabel, tension filling the air between us. For my part, I didn't like the way the Witch looking at my kitten. "Whatever you're thinking, Deg, stop it."

He forced his gaze away from Mabel. "You have to

admit none of that should have happened, LA. And the cat should be dead."

In desperation, I dug deep for a possible explanation. "Maybe you somehow healed her when you healed Mandy."

To my shock, he considered the suggestion. "The only way that happened is if she was somehow attached to Mandy."

"Or the energy got caught up in the rug and travelled to her," Mandy offered.

I felt my eyes go wide. "That could be it, Deg." The thought made me happy, especially when he finally stopped looking at the kitten as if she were somehow responsible for the attack. "I guess that's possible." He reached for the cat and she hissed, wriggling to escape my arms. I settled her to the rug and Mabel bounced over to Mandy, winding happily between her legs. The Witch scooped her up and nuzzled her soft throat.

"Looks like she prefers women," I told Deg when he frowned.

Shrugging, he seemed to dismiss the dis. "We need to get to work."

"I need more potion," Mandy said.

"And I need to get this little one back to the sanctuary and check on the others."

Deg nodded but he was already seated in the center of the rug, legs crossed and eyes closed. He placed his hands out to his sides, palms down, and sent his peculiar silver-toned energy downward.

Mandy reluctantly handed Mabel back to me, her gaze speculative. "I've always wanted a cat."

The question in her statement was clear. But I chose to ignore it. I wasn't ready to think about rehoming the kittens. Especially Mabel. There was something about the little feline that tugged at me. I wanted more time to figure out what I was going to do with her. "I'll see you in a few minutes."

What I didn't tell her was that it would probably be a bit longer, because I had something else in mind than just checking in on my visitors to make sure they were okay. I intended to question them more thoroughly, to find out if they had a sense for what had invaded our little sanctuary, first that morning and moments before, through the portal.

Animals were extremely sensitive to energy pulses through the air. In fact they were virtual magic barometers. I wanted to get my sanctuary cats' perceptions of the entity before we tried to tackle it again.

However, I wasn't ready for what I found when I opened the door to the sanctuary and stepped inside.

Sliding to a halt, I stopped breathing.

Something waited for me inside. Something dark and deadly.

I must have been holding Mabel too tightly because she squirmed in my arms, giving a plaintiff little yowl as I held on tight.

I fully intended to turn around and deposit the kitten safely in the house before running to warn Deg and Mandy we had an intruder, but the kitten had other ideas. When she couldn't get free she bit down on my finger. Hard. And I released her with a gasp of pain. She dropped lightly to her paws on the grass and skittered away, disappearing behind a trio of boulders situated beneath a wide beam of silvery moonlight.

She was probably going to make sure her brothers were okay. I assumed they were hiding somewhere, no doubt terrified.

Reaching for the energy at my core, I pulled it forward enough to allow my claws to spring free. Then, hiding my hands in the pockets of my skirt, I moved into the park-like room, my gaze scanning for the invader. As I looked, I listened for my visitors, hoping to determine that they were all right.

I immediately picked up several heartbeats, scattered around the room. One was up high in a clump of trees that reached toward the thirty-foot, clear glass ceiling above my head. Two were muffled, no doubt coming from the tunnel I'd dug beneath the sanctuary for those who just liked to hide.

Three heartbeats pounded in fast rhythm behind the boulders. My guess had been correct. Mabel had found her siblings and they were hunkered down out of sight.

There should have been more, but I surmised a few of my guests had made use of the cat door at the back of the large space and were out and about, hopefully clear of danger.

A shadow moved across the floor in front of me and I stopped, my heartbeat in my throat and a heaviness in my chest that told me I'd forgotten to breathe.

I carefully pulled air into my lungs, my gaze locked on the large, amorphous shape moving toward me across the space.

The shadow seemed to flex, spreading one moment and then contracting, becoming more tall than wide. It was not humanoid, nor was it shaped like any animal I'd ever encountered. But one thing was certain. Whatever it was, it was giving off a menacing aura that had gooseflesh popping up along my arms.

My nose stung under the stench of sulfur. It was a scent that shouldn't exist in the sanctuary. All of my guests were actual felines. There were no shapeshifters in the room. Which meant there was a magic user inside my home. One that I hadn't invited in.

"Who's here?"

I felt the alarm of my guests uptick at the sound of my voice, followed by random thoughts of movement. What I didn't know was if they were thinking about fleeing *me* or my uninvited guest.

Some of my newer guests hadn't yet decided if they liked me or not.

The shadow flared outward, growing round, and then stopped a few yards from my feet. I felt a surge in the collective energy of the space. Filled with dread, I gathered magic in my fingertips and waited.

LA?

I jumped at the sound of Deg's voice in my head, frowning. *Get out of my head.*

The shadow flexed and rolled, clearly drawn to my discomfort.

What's wrong? I feel your fear.

I'm in the middle of something. I'll tell you later. I ruthlessly walled off any further communication with him. It was strange to confer in my head with another human. I generally only managed it with animals or other shapeshifters in their animal form.

I kept my gaze locked on the shadow, magic spitting from my clawed fingers. "Tell me who you are or face the consequences."

Since I was all but drooling on myself with fear at the moment, I wasn't sure what consequences I could threaten the intruder with. On the positive side, maybe he or she was afraid of drool.

The shadow seemed to close in on itself and then grow so long and thin it all but disappeared.

The light left the far end of the sanctuary and darkness oozed in my direction. I almost peed myself before I realized it was just a bank of clouds moving overhead, beyond the glass ceiling.

That was when it clicked in my brain. The shadow I was seeing wasn't something stalking me from the ether.

Very slowly, holding my breath and with fingers ready to throw energy, I looked upward, to the gnarled tree branch hanging about ten feet above my head.

And I saw it.

Whatever it was, it was grotesquely round and misshapen, oozing hostility, with an aggressive gaze that glowed down on me with menace.

CHAPTER THIRTEEN

*A*ctually, the eyes just seemed menacing because their owner was clearly peeved. Her tail snapped angrily from side to side behind her, no doubt the cause of the constantly morphing shadow she threw on the ground.

Hello, cher.

Posh. I almost peed myself. Why didn't you tell me you were here? Then it occurred to me she shouldn't have been able to recognize me in my human form. I narrowed my gaze on the big cat. *How did you find me?*

Her wide face looked as indignant as a cat's face could. *You don't think I knew what you were?* She jumped down from the branch, hitting the ground with a weighty thump. *I lied when I said I was going to do my rounds, cher. I followed you to the barrier.*

A ribbon of unease slithered through me. *And why would you do that?*

The cat's shoulders flexed upward as if she were shrugging. *I had my reasons.*

I had a sudden thought. *Did you follow me into the park?*

That's what I said, cher.

No, she hadn't said that. I frowned. *Then you saw the body I found?*

Posh drew herself upright, her tail snapping angrily. *I saw that you found her, yes.*

Something about the way she said it... *You knew she was there, didn't you?*

A weary sigh filled my head. *I thought you'd never come, cher. I've been sending out feelers for days.*

I don't understand.

I found Tabby hours before you did. I'd been looking for her since she disappeared.

Why didn't you just tell me where she was?

I didn't know if I could trust you. I had to see for myself that you meant well.

I sighed. *I understand.*

The big cat hung her head, sadness oozing from her despondent form. *She was my friend.*

I'm sorry, Posh. I really am.

She swung her head from side to side. *Someone's declared war on the Familiars. We need to find him and shut him down.*

I lowered myself to a rock so I wasn't towering over her. *Do you have any idea who it is?*

Only broadly. Her strangely colored gaze lifted to mine. *I think it's a Witch.*

Why do you think that?

She shrugged again. *Because it's obviously somebody really powerful. With skills Familiars don't have.*

Her words scraped my ego raw. I'd spent my life proclaiming that I didn't need to subjugate myself to a

Witch because I was every bit as powerful as one. But for me it wasn't just ego. I'd observed my best friend being dominated by a Witch, belittled and held in contempt until she had no feelings of self-worth left. I'd watched helplessly as a once vibrant life dimmed and faded away. I vowed then that I'd never allow myself to fall into the trap. It hadn't been easy. I'd had to go against centuries of Familiar - Witch practices to do it. But I'd been proud to be the master of my own fate and I pledged every day never to look back. *I think you're underestimating my people.*

Don't get me wrong. I know there are powerful Familiars. Your mother and grandmamma to name a couple, but there's a difference. Familiars can be really good at one or two things. Sometimes even more. A Witch carries the markers for many types of magic, from light to dark and everything in between.

I had to concede her point. *Okay, I'll give you that.*

She nodded. *And this magic user has not only stolen the web, but he's made it his bitch, cher. That's some phenomenal energy there.*

A soft mewling sound had me dropping my gaze to find Mabel rubbing against the rock I was sitting on. "Hey, cutie."

The tiny kitten brushed against the hand I lowered to her and then proceeded to wind herself, purring loudly, around my feet. She stopped when she came within a foot of Posh and locked gazes with the other cat, her tiny form relaxed but still.

Hullo, child.

Mabel's tail twitched and she turned to look up at me. *It's okay, sweetie. She's a friend.*

The baby dropped to her butt, watching Posh's every move.

After a minute, Posh stirred. *You need to teach the kid some manners, LA.*

She's not quite herself, I'm afraid. She got caught in the crossfire with whoever we're tracking a while ago.

And she survived? Posh's regard turned more intense. *There's not much to her.*

And you say I'm rude.

I blinked as a high-pitched, child-like voice infiltrated my thoughts.

Posh's tail twitched. *It ain't polite to stare.*

It's not polite to call me small either.

Why ever not? You are small, cher. C'est un fait.

It's a fact you shouldn't mention because it's rude, Mabel insisted.

Given in her trebly, childish voice, the kitten's words were more than adorable. I couldn't help smiling.

Posh's husky laugh filtered through my mind. *She a feisty one, I'll give 'er dat.*

Mabel is much stronger than she looks, Posh. I gave the kitten a soft smile. *She saved my friend's life.*

You friends wid a Witch? If the renewed agitation of Posh's tail was any indication, she was not pleased.

I just met her but, yes. Mandy and I are friends. Of a sort.

Posh shook her head. *C'est malheureux.*

It's not unfortunate at all. I need all the help I can get to find this guy.

Actually, that's why I'm here. I know where he is.

Excitement swelled. I jumped off the rock, causing Mabel to give a panicked leap sideways. *Why didn't you say so? I'll go get the others.*

Dat's not what I had in mind, cher. Dis is a job for Familiars. No witches allowed.

But I can't do this alone, I argued.

You won't have to, cher. I'm goin' ta help.

I appreciate your willingness to put yourself in danger, Posh... I shook my head.

I can do dis, cher. I got my own magic.

But you're just a cat...

Now who's bein' rude, cher?

I'm sorry but it's true.

There's a lot more to me dan meets da eye, Posh insisted.

Mabel approached the other cat, leaning closer to give her a sniff. *She's right, Miss LA. There's something off about her.*

Not off, child. Special.

I shook my head. *I'm sure you're a very special feline but...*

The cat lumbered to her feet. *Maybe this will help.* Her round form gave a violent jerk and I blinked, alarm spiking. She stretched forward, her thick legs extended out in front of her and her head down between them. A wave of movement slipped over her wide frame, rolling her fur from the base of her tail to her broad head.

Cracking sounds emerged.

My hand flew to my mouth as I realized what was happening. But I couldn't believe what I was seeing. How could I have missed it?

Posh's big form twisted upward, her paws slapping the air in front of her as her back end bent and elongated. Her tail disappeared with a pop and sparks erupted as her body expanded upward.

A sulfurous cloud filled the air between us and, when it finally cleared, I gasped.

A naked woman stood where the cat had been. A woman whose name I'd never bothered to learn when I'd met her as a human. "You're the receptionist at *Familiar, Inc.*"

"Yes."

"You're a shifter? How is it possible I didn't know?"

The woman gave me a smile. "How is it possible nobody knows you're a shifter?"

Okay, she had me there. Then realization dawned. "You're a tracker too?"

"I am."

I thought about it a moment and then nodded. "That explains how you found me here."

"You would think so, wouldn't you?"

I frowned. "What's that supposed to mean?"

"It means I didn't track you here. I was sent here by someone close to you."

Fear slipped up my spine. "Who?"

"Your mother. And we need to hurry. She and Celeste are in grave danger. It might already be too late."

CHAPTER FOURTEEN

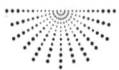

*W*e stood looking through the metal spires of the massive gate. The building beyond reminded me of a haunted castle. It wasn't a house. Even in my cat form, when everything looked bigger, I recognized that it was way too big for that. With its blackened stone exterior and odd, circular portico, the thing looked more like a citadel than a house.

A cold breeze wafted over Posh and me as we sat staring at the foreboding place. The coming storm was heavy in the air, the scent of ozone thickening by the moment. So it was no surprise, a moment later, when lightning speared the night sky above the intimidating structure.

Are those bats flying around up there? I asked Posh. *This is like something straight out of a horror film.*

It 'pears dis killer like ta put on da show.

I glanced over at the big cat sitting next to me. Posh scanned the area carefully, her enormous form completely still. I understood the seriousness of the task ahead. It would be a miracle if we even survived. Still, there was something that had been bothering me. Something I had to know. So I asked. *How come you only have a Cajun accent in cat form?* I wouldn't ask why she was so much...erm... fluffier too. That would just be rude.

She slid a narrowed glance my way. 'Tis da way of things, cher. And just so's ya know, y'all sound like a bimbo in fur.

Said fur stood straight on end with outrage. *I do not!* But even as I protested, my mind registered the high-pitched, sexy drawl of my voice. I'd never even noticed it before. In my brain I'd always thought I was me no matter what form I took.

Mm, hm. You sho do. And you dat much nicer as a cat too.

I shook my head, suddenly anxious to change the subject. *What is this place, anyway?*

This here's the old, historic Hotel Xavier. It been closed for decades but it was quite da place in its day.

Xavier? I thought of the X cut into Tabitha's delicate hand and sadness flared through me, pulling the air from my lungs. *Of course.* She'd been trying to tell me where her killer was.

I gave it another careful look, noting the details in the roofline and the enormous, broken fountain in the bricked, circular drive at the front. If I squinted really hard, I could almost see the grand structure it had once been. *Cool.*

It were built on a Ley line and dere used ta be all manner o' goin's on here. Folks reported run-ins with vampire-like creatures, men who transformed into wolves, and more than the usual share of ghostly goings on.

If I'd been human I would have grinned. In my current

state the smile came out as a purr. *Sounds pretty normal to me.*

Me too. But I ain't a pale, stick-limbed human.

I chuckled.

Come on, cher. We got work ta do. Posh slipped a thick leg between the spires and somehow managed to compress herself enough to slip through. I quickly followed, but despite my determination to get to my family, the oily energy pulsating around the place as we got closer dimmed my enthusiasm and slowed my steps.

Each stride forward seemed mired in quicksand, every movement required an excess of strength. I was soon panting with the effort and my pulse pounded so hard I was afraid I was going to stroke out.

Posh wasn't faring any better. With her added bulk, she soon became unsteady with weariness. We stopped to rest in a row of bushes that edged the circular drive. I guessed the prickly things had probably been neatly trimmed once upon a time, but in their current state they were little more than spikey barriers, tangled and over-grown so that they were nearly impossible to pass through.

I tried to ignore them as I lay down in the icy dirt next to Posh. The big cat's chest heaved from the effort of approaching the killer's hidey hole.

Clearly the place had been heavily warded.

Even as I had the thought a sharp pain speared my side. I gave off a soft yowl and bent away from the pain, only to encounter a similar sting on my thigh.

Posh hissed softly and jumped to her feet. I turned in time to see a prickly finger of bush snap out and pierce her in the chest. Blood dotted her coat and her eyes were wide.

Two more branches sliced through my skin and one wrapped around my leg, yanking hard and flinging me to the ground. I lost track of the number of times I was stabbed by the horrid greenery. Posh writhed and yowled beside me, clearly going through the same agony I was.

We need to get out of here! I panted. Unfortunately, another prickly branch had found my throat and was quickly closing off my air.

Posh's situation wasn't any better. One of the enchanted vines had her around the middle and was squeezing hard. Her strange colored eyes were bulging. *Shift...* she gasped out as blood spurted from the place where the thorns dug into her body.

She didn't have to tell me twice. Though I knew it was going to hurt a lot, when I had more skin for the branches to grab, I also knew I'd have a better chance if I were bigger.

With a yowl of pain, we both reached for our transformative magics and shifted, bumping against each other as our bodies grew and thrashed.

Agony wrapped me in a prickly embrace and I bit down on my screams so I wouldn't give away our position. As soon as I was me again, I crawled on hands and knees through the rabid greenery, my skin ripping as I moved.

I shoved my top half free and thought I'd made it. But a large branch shot out and wrapped around my ankle, ripping me backward again. The bushes shook as Posh fought her way out, yelping with pain.

I kicked out to try to extricate myself and felt the

branch loosen. But just as I thought I was going to make it free, the thing tightened around me, tearing fresh holes in my skin, and yanked hard.

I flew backward, thorns ripping the flesh of my thighs, and screamed as fire-like pain sliced through me. My fingertips scrabbled desperately in the frozen dirt for something to stop my return to the hedge.

It was no good. There was nothing for me to grab. Heart pounding with terror, I felt myself being slowly and inextricably dragged back inside the deadly bush. Another branch snaked out and grabbed my other ankle.

There was a flash inside the bushes and Posh flew out, sailing overhead with her arms and legs flailing. She hit the ground behind me with a heavy thud and lay there, unmoving.

Giving up on trying to anchor myself, I rolled to my back and fired energy into the branch surrounding one ankle. With nothing to slow me down, I surged more quickly toward the hedge. But at least I'd gotten one ankle free. I quickly killed the second vine but, before I could scrabble away, two more branches found me.

Rage replaced terror as pain and frustration combined to create a potent cocktail. I yanked my magic forward and, with a scream that reverberated through the area around the old hotel, I sent it flying, watching in surprise as it left my hands in a white hot wash of energy that lit up the offending vegetation, turning it to smoking stalks in seconds.

I quickly scrambled away and then dropped, lying on my back for a moment to regain my breath.

"Remind me never to piss you off," Posh said from behind me.

I twisted my head to look over at her. "You okay?"

She shoved slowly to her feet, groaning. "Yeah. But we need to move. I'm pretty sure we've lost the element of surprise."

I reluctantly climbed to my feet too. "Sorry about the whole primal scream thing."

She shrugged. "Anger's potent magic. It certainly gave your power an edge."

We both scanned a final look over the smoldering remains of the bush and then, without another word, turned on our heels and started running toward the blackened face of the scary building.

We ran along the front of the big structure, taking care to avoid the overgrown bushes hugging the stone façade. The windows loomed overhead, making me feel exposed. They were like giant blackened eyeballs spying on us as we ran.

The feeling of being watched spurred me to run faster, and brought the hairs up on the back of my neck. Posh must have felt the same because she kept looking over her shoulder.

At the end of the building we stopped and peered around the corner. A brisk, cold wind shrieked past us, filled with the stench of the grave. "Where do you suppose that's coming from?" I asked Posh.

"As far as I know there aren't any cemeteries back there."

I shivered as another moist blast scoured over me. "Then somebody's using death magic." The realization made my stomach tighten with fear. I couldn't help wondering what unfortunate Familiar had been sacrificed. "We need to get in there."

"That's the idea," Posh said as she scanned a look toward the roofline. She turned to me. "Can you climb?"

I realized she was referring to the tree hugging the wall. "Let's do it." I focused my thoughts on my transformative magic and rode out the quick pain of the shift. As a cat, the night surrounding me had an entirely different taste and color. But the rotting stench still smelled like death. Only worse.

I leapt onto the rough-barked trunk of the big old tree and scampered up, hitting the first branch and quickly moving up until I found a branch that overhung the tattered roof. I leapt onto the broken tile and gave a panicked yowl as the shingles shifted under my paws, sending me sliding nearly to the edge before my claws found purchase.

Posh hesitated on the branch, watching me as I carefully made my way back to the peak. *Tread carefully,* I told her. With her added bulk I had to believe she was in more danger than I was of sending the broken and rotted tiles into a slide.

She stepped carefully off the branch, keeping it between her and the edge, and moved quickly toward the center. I wondered if she knew where she was going. She certainly seemed as if she did. We came upon a wide, concrete chimney and Posh stopped. *This is our best entry point,* she told me with a straight, if cat-like face.

I jumped up and eyed the deep, constricted opening. Then I narrowed my gaze on her belly. Posh bristled, literally, making her look even more round.

Don't worry about me, cher, just scurry on down dat chimney. I'll be right behind you.

Maybe you should go first. In case you get...erm...

If she had hands and hips at that moment I was pretty sure she'd have connected them. As it was, she had to make do with a swishing tail and a narrowed gaze. *Den what? Wid me jammed in da openin' y'all won't be able ta get down either. At least if y'all go first den one of us will make it down.*

I sighed. After we'd rescued the trapped Familiars Posh and I were going to have a little talk about her eating habits as a cat. It was hard to be a super sleuth when your size restricted your sleuthing. She was just darn lucky the calories she consumed as a cat didn't translate to her human form. *Okay. Wish me luck.* I started to climb inside and stopped. *Do we have any idea where this ends up?*

Nah. But it don't matter. Dis place is huge. Dere's like no chance it will take us to the exact place he's holding them.

Famous last words. I should have known when Posh said them that they spelled my doom. I really needed to trust my instincts. Because if I had, I might have been saved a lot of bladder weakening terror in the coming moments.

CHAPTER FIFTEEN

I took a deep, bracing breath and leapt. As soon as I started to fall I went spread-eagled, using my claws against the tar-covered brick to slow my descent. Still, I was moving at quite a clip when I found the bottom and, if it hadn't been for the pile of ash breaking my fall my landing would have been much harder.

I only wish the charred timber hadn't still been sizzling hot from a recent fire.

The smoldering center of the ashes flared and snapped as I hit, sending a fine, gray cloud into the air to cover my fur. The fiery remains erupted into flame beneath me.

I shot straight into the air on a yowl of pain and landed outside the fireplace, my sore paws finding dusty brick that was warmed from the fire.

I sat down and began licking the pads of my feet, soothing the pain as best I could. Still, when I stood again, the pain shot up my legs and took my breath away. I considered shifting to heal, but knew I'd have a better chance of finding my prey as a cat. So I tried to ignore it as best I could and moved away from the fire, scenting the space I found myself in.

It appeared to be a large room, its edges lost in the deep shadows lurking behind the fading glow of the fire. Beyond the brick the floor softened under a filthy red carpet that sported a diamond pattern. The occasional piece of furniture showed gilding beneath the grime and I figured the big space had once been an elegant party room of some sort. Broken plaster hung from age darkened beams far above my head. In the center of the lofty ceiling was the remains of a large plaster medallion which had probably surrounded the base of a chandelier. The walls were covered in something dark that hung in tatters. Probably wallpaper. The blackened paper had been worn away by time and, from the rusty stains trailing down the torn surface, I presumed water had been creeping over the walls for some time.

Silence spread ominously around me.

The combined stench of filth, mildew, and mouse droppings assailed my feline senses.

Despite no visual evidence of a threat I was on high alert. My fur stood on end and a low growl simmered at the base of my throat. There was an unnatural element to the lack of sound and visual clues.

I had little doubt there was magic afoot.

And to make things worse, I could still feel someone watching me.

Behind me, a prolonged screeching sound was punctuated by a deep, alarmed growl and a meaty thump that sent another cloud of ash into the room.

Posh yelped and flew out of the smoldering remains,

hitting the brick floor and sliding sideways about three feet before coming up hard against a heavy wooden table leg.

Her fur smoldered and the tip of her thick tail flared briefly before extinguishing with a soft pop.

I hurried over and nudged her with a paw. *Are you okay?*

For a long moment Posh didn't move or respond. She lay in an untidy bump on the floor, perfectly still. I was starting to think she'd knocked herself out on the table when she finally stirred. *I've been better, cher.*

Nothing's broken? I asked, my gaze sliding around the room.

I don't think so.

Then get up and let's keep moving. I think somebody's watching us. It's giving me the heebies.

She groaned softly as she pushed to her wide paws. *This place has been warded. Nothing we're seeing is real.*

Ya think? My gaze still scanning nervously, I nudged her on the shoulder, gently prodding her toward the space beneath the table. *I've seen places like this before,* I told Posh.

Yeah, in a Disney cartoon. This here's a monster's lair. If I'm not mistaken, that bowl up there's filled with gruel.

I would have chuckled except she wasn't wrong. Somebody was playing with our minds. *Come on, let's keep moving. We can unravel the warding as we go. I have a suspicion things are going to get more interesting before they get better.*

Sometimes I think I might be prescient. Most times I regret it a little.

Occasionally, like in the next moment, I regretted it a lot.

As we moved away from the protection of the big table, the shadows burst open and a pair of massive, hairy feet pounded toward us, accompanied by a wall-shaking roar.

A mountain of unwashed, pocked and malformed flesh stomped across the room, hands as big as car tires reaching downward.

Run! I screamed at Posh.

I didn't need to tell her twice. The meaty feline took off like a shot, her round form seeming to skim across the top of the dirty carpet and her legs moving so fast they were a blur. I wasn't far behind but, as she disappeared through a wide doorway in the nearest wall, a massive hand slammed down between us and hot, putrid breath scoured my back.

I yowled in surprise and skidded to a halt, barely keeping from slamming into the side of the enormous hand.

"Got ya!" a gravelly, nightmarish voice boomed overhead. And I felt the warm, strong grip of fingers as long as my entire human body wrap around me.

In a panic, I did the only thing I could think to do. I shifted, quickly and without thought.

The result was painful for everyone concerned. I felt as if someone had grabbed each of my four limbs and was pulling me apart into quarters.

The giant apparently felt the burn of my energy because he released me with a roar of pain and stumbled backward a couple of steps, holding his hand.

I hit the unforgiving carpet hard when he dropped me, pain radiating through my sacroiliac and wrenching my neck. But I didn't stop to think about what I might have damaged in the five foot free fall. There was no time. Already, the putrid smelling giant was lifting his shaggy head, his beady, slightly crossed eyes glaring down at me.

As I shoved to my feet and took off running, I couldn't help thinking that, whoever was pulling the magic strings in that cursed place had a very sick sense of humor.

I only hoped the final joke wasn't on me.

I plunged through the same door Posh had escaped through and dodged sideways, looking for a way out as the floor shook under the giant's heavy footsteps.

I stood there panting like a puppy in August, my heart slamming against my ribs, and watched the door with a sense of horrified foreboding. I expected him to crash through the opening and be on me again in mere seconds. Dread overcame me, locking my muscles and making it hard to think.

I knew I had to keep moving or die. But something kept me rooted to the spot.

Suddenly the pounding stopped.

I paused, wondering if he was trying to wait me out. But nothing came through the door.

Okay, I thought. I wouldn't look a gift horse—or monster—in the mouth. Shoving away from the wall I was cowering against, I took off running. There was no sign of Posh anywhere and that worried me. I figured she had to be nearby, but I was beginning to realize we'd entered a house of horrors. And It would only take one wrong move...

Even as I had the thought, a strident scream rent the air, the sound so feral and filled with terror I wasn't sure if it was human or animal.

A sudden fear sprang up inside me. Had that been my

mother screaming? Or Celeste? What if the Witch who had them knew I was coming for him and decided to send me a message.

On that thought I dug in, determined to find them more quickly. Because if there was one thing I'd figured out in the years dealing with magical beings, they could be very good if so inclined, but when they went bad... well...I knew there'd be no reasoning with the owner of the house of horrors I found myself in.

I plunged through a door and was immediately smacked violently across the face by something large and wet. With a yelp of surprise, I dodged sideways and spun, energy spitting from my fingertips. I stared, panting, at a wide, dew-covered leaf, attached to a large plant whose palm-like leaves waved in a soft, balmy breeze.

I frowned. Glancing around the space, I realized I was surrounded by the things, as well as a variety of actual palm trees whose branches fluttered high above my head. Humid warmth baked me, bringing about my own dew that sprang up to cover my face and moisten my palms. The place smelled verdant and clean, with a tang of salt water in the distance.

Above my head a bright sun burned yellow and hot, surrounded by a pretty blue sky filled with wispy clouds.

"What the...?"

The scream sounded again and I looked up as something huge and colorful dove toward my head. The bird's enormous hooked beak clacked in warning as it passed within inches of my no doubt tangled red head. A large, shiny glop of something hit the ground an inch from my big toe.

The huge bird spread its wings and they looked to be

twenty feet across. Its clawed feet were bigger than my head and looked deadly enough to kill. The monster-sized parrot didn't slow or turn back. I got the distinct impression it was running from something. But what would a bird bigger than me be running from?

Unfortunately, I was about to find out.

The ground shuddered beneath my feet. The sun disappeared behind a dense gray cloud and I shivered as the breeze sliding through the vegetation turned cold and sour with menace. All around me, moist green plants shivered and bent, flinging drops of water into the air as they sprang back behind the wind.

My ears popped and there was no sound. I could still see the movement around me, feel the change in the weather, but it was like I was in a bubble.

Apart from it all.

Into the sudden silence, a new sound emerged. It was nothing I could identify. There was a heaviness to it...an ever-changing presence that affected everything in its path but seemed to touch nothing at all.

I focused hard and finally realized what I was hearing. It was the meaty sound of something being dragged across the ground.

The room grew even darker...so dark I could no longer make out distinct shapes. Only movement permeated my sudden blindness.

And there was a lot of that.

A harsh breeze carried with it the rancid stench of something I didn't recognize. I sent out my senses to search for it and found it much too quickly.

Right behind me.

Sucking in a terrified gasp, I whipped around to face

whatever stalked me, my heart pounding. A round, brown object slammed into me, hitting me hard, right in my gut.

A coconut.

Agony flared as the hairy missile thumped to the ground.

I tried to breathe around the pain but no air would come. My screeching attempts to pull air into my lungs sounded terrifyingly loud in the ominous silence.

My knees buckled and I went down.

The hiss was loud...drawn out and terrifying. A silvery arrow flashed downward from the darkened sky and I thought it was lightning.

It wasn't lightning.

I scanned a gaze upward. Way, way, up, to the spot where the cloud blocked the sun, I swallowed hard, my eyes going wide.

Two bright yellow orbs stared down at me, lidless and dead. The gaze was coldly calculating, assessing, like a lion considering the best way to devour its prey. And as it slowly lowered toward the ground I realized two things that made my blood run cold.

One, that was no cloud blocking the sun.

And two, if I didn't start running right that minute, I was about to become monster kibble.

CHAPTER SIXTEEN

*W*hy did it have to be a snake? I hated snakes. I was terrified of them. Especially when they had heads that were ten feet wide. With a head that big I could only imagine how big the thing's body was. Suddenly the frantic movement of the plants as far as my eye could see made perfect sense.

The monster was all around me. Coiled.

And, unless I totally missed my guess, I was standing dead center of the coil.

Just flaming craptastic!

The eyes narrowed slightly, the head shooting up, and I realized it was about to strike. I dove into the under-brush and yanked my energy forward, quickly morphing into my cat just as the massive fangs ripped into the ground where I'd been standing. All around me the vege-tation thrashed and bent as the thing's dense length snapped around.

A tree crashed down in front of me and I leapt side-ways, taking off in a new direction.

Another tree collapsed, landing just inches behind me and flinging coconut cannon balls into the surrounding greenery.

The vegetation just ahead split and a nasty looking wild pig dashed out, tusks glistening with something I didn't want to identify.

Panic swirled as the pig ran right at me, but as I leapt up onto a gnarled tree and scrambled upward, the thing ran mindlessly onward as if it hadn't even seen me.

A beat later I heard its scream as it presumably met the snake.

I shuddered, climbing faster. Usually getting higher made me feel safe, but I couldn't escape the feeling of being shepherded to a specific place. Especially as the tree I was climbing shuddered and started to fall.

As it crashed downward I leapt to the next tree in the line, risking a quick look back to find part of the snake's thick, black body coiled around the tree I'd left behind. As I watched in horror, the enormous tree was pulled from the ground, thick roots and all, and flung in my direction.

I couldn't outrun the monstrous snake. It was too big, too comfortable in its surroundings. Panic made a sour taste in my mouth. My heart beat painfully against my chest. My breath stuttered from between trembling lips. I slammed to a stop as the giant head appeared just above the tree, glowing eyes searching the area for me. Pressing against the trunk, I tried to make myself small and prayed the thing couldn't hear my heart pounding.

A forked tongue as wide as my arm slithered out from between yellow, scaled lips, testing the air to find me. I closed my eyes and tried to come up with a plan.

I could try to mask my presence with a cloaking spell.

But magic leaves behind a distinct signature that could be traced. I didn't know if a magical snake monster could sense magic. If it could, it would be like coating myself with a tasty brown sauce for the snake's pleasure.

I could keep running, hoping I'd get really lucky. So far luck was *not* my lady. If I could find a doorway out of the current horror show maybe I'd have a chance. Looking around, I saw nothing resembling a door. As far as I could tell I'd dropped into a prehistoric world with no exit.

The forked appendage slipped through the densely leaved branch over my head and passed within inches of my shoulder. I cowered against the trunk and held my breath.

Far down below me, wide leaves shifted as the thing's coils tightened. I couldn't escape the feeling that the snake knew exactly where I was and was just playing with me.

The tree shuddered violently and I nearly fell off. I sounded a panicked yowl before I could squelch it, my claws digging deeply into the hard wood.

The tree shuddered again and I looked down as the snake's enormous black body slithered around the trunk and wrenched, shifting the dirt at its base. I was seconds away from having the tree literally yanked out from under me.

I held on as the tree was juddered several more times, my claws aching from the effort. I had to move, but I had no idea where.

There were no trees close enough to leap to. Finally, as the tree convulsed so violently it dislodged my rear claws and left me hanging, I realized I had only one choice. I sent energy into my front claws and used it to pull myself back up onto the tree and then, as it started to rip from the soil, scampered toward the ground as fast as I could. Gritting my teeth, tasting fear like acid in my throat, I leapt onto the meaty coils and sprang off before the snake could loosen itself and grab hold. I hit the torn ground and pushed off even as the soil slipped away from my claws, plunging back into the shivering vegetation at full speed.

A soft rattling sound was all the warning I got that the tail was coming my way. It slashed past my nose, barely missing me, and immediately swung back and smacked me hard in the back. I flew into the air, heading directly for a thick palm with ragged, painfully sharp bark.

I braced myself, knowing it was going to hurt, a lot, when I hit.

Eyes squeezed closed, I slammed into something hard. Strangely it didn't hurt as much as I'd expected. In fact it felt kind of leathery. And smelled like…

Sulfur!

I opened my eyes and looked up, up, up into a demonic countenance, the fierce red gaze blazing like fire in a handsome black face. A thick cap of shiny black hair swept away from the well-known face and caressed a pair of very sharp horns before falling in perfect waves down the back of Brock's perfect head.

He had to be ten feet tall in his current form.

He held a clawed, black finger up to his lips and shoved me behind him. "Stay here," he growled before taking off at a run. He leapt into the air and thirty-foot-wide, jagged-edged wings unfurled from his back, pounding rhythmically as he rose above the trees.

I stood at the base of the palm tree in shocked silence. I'd never seen Brock in his demonic form and was surprised that he was still strangely beautiful and utterly terrifying at the same time.

What was he doing there? And how had he found me? But more importantly, what the heck was he going to do about the enormous pair of future snakeskin boots that was stalking me?

Quick as a wink, I got my answer.

The snake's massive head whipped out, mouth spread wide, and snatched Brock out of the air. His ten-foot length and much of his wingspan disappeared inside the thing's maw.

I gave a scream, stepping forward in panic. I reached out an arm and realized with a start that I'd returned to my human form without realizing it. Sometimes when I panicked I leaked magic and things happened that I didn't plan.

I'd suffered pre-mature magiculation.

How embarrassing.

High above my head the battle raged. Brock had managed to release his arms and the snake's head was whipping from side to side as the demon shot fire toward its eyes and clawed at the flesh enfolding him. I stood in a horrified trance, unable to move as Brock fought a battle for his life. It seemed there should be something I could do to help. But I had no idea what.

Then it hit me. What Brock needed was a distraction. I could certainly do that.

I started to run, forcing my feet to move directly toward the snake. As I got closer my sightlines changed. Because of the denseness of the vegetation surrounding its coils, I lost sight of the rampaging monster for a moment. But I could see the trees wobbling and going down under the thing's weight, so I headed for the devastation.

I knew I was close when a loud scraping sound erupted behind me. I turned just in time to see a palm tree sliding across the broken and mashed greenery, directly at me.

I leapt off the ground, barely clearing the huge tree, and landed behind the meaty band of the snake's tail, which was propelling it.

A flash of insight filled my brain and I knew what to do.

Lifting my hands, I focused on the tree, and shot a bolt of pure, white energy into it. The palm flared brightly and burst into flame, the supercharged blaze licking hungrily over the monster's black flesh.

The creature stilled, the jungle going silent for just a beat, and then stiffened. The tail lifted high above my head and crashed down mere inches away. I started to run as it lifted again.

The world exploded around me. Chunks of leaves and tree detonated into the air, sliced my skin and speckled the surrounding area.

I ran as fast as I could, blindly shoving through wet leaves and leaping broken brush in a frantic attempt to escape the thrashing monster.

Above it all was a strange hissing sound, like the air being released from a giant dirigible. My lungs seized over the sulfur stench. Brock's wings once again beat the air high above my head. I was happy he'd gotten free.

But I had a new problem.

As I ran pell-mell through the prehistoric nightmare, something dropped heavily between two trees directly ahead.

Its eyes blazing with rage.

Its deadly lips slipping open to test the air between us with a slimy tongue.

The thing focused its wrath on me.

A huge form lowered from the sky between me and the snake. Brock's back was to me, his wings lazily drubbing the air, and his body was hard with tension. He didn't turn as he spoke in my mind. *Get out of here, LA.*

I'm not leaving you alone with this thing.

You need to go.

I won't.

His sigh filled my brain, throbbing with frustration. *Damn stubborn Familiar.*

Whatever. Just tell me what to do.

I already did. But you won't listen. So at least go hide somewhere so I can concentrate on kicking this thing's...well it doesn't actually have an ass does it?

I chuckled darkly. *It's all ass, except for the head and that rattly thing on the end of its tail.*

The snake's tongue shot toward Brock and he sliced energy over it, cutting off the last five feet.

The monster's head twisted upward, clearly incensed, and then slammed down in front of Brock, sending him flying.

Brock!

Go, LA!

I started to object. I never got the chance. A rectangle of light opened up behind me and, before I could even turn to see what it was, a pair of hands grabbed my shoulders and yanked me through the opening.

Into a different kind of hell.

CHAPTER SEVENTEEN

I hit a long form that was icy cold to the touch and wrapped in something rough and sticky. I jerked away, whipping around to see what I needed to kill. Rotating violently from my touch, a mummy-shaped form hung by a long, hairy string from the rafters. The thing was shaped like a banana, narrow on both ends and wider in the middle. With a horrified twitch I realized the rough wrap was slightly translucent. If I looked really hard I could just make out the long, bony shapes of fingers. A moment later I realized two slender arms were crossed over a flattened chest and my gaze lifted slowly, even as I took a step back, my heart pounding with dread.

A pair of pale blue eyes stared back at me, unblinking. I gave a horrified shout and stumbled backward, only to come up against another cocoon. Yelping, I dodged sideways and hit another. I ping ponged my way down an entire line of the things before I found the courage to stand still and breathe through the horrified slamming of my heart against my ribs.

I recognized a few of the faces behind the webbing that held them in a deathly grip. They were some of the missing familiars. Some I barely knew. Some I considered friends. But as realization hit, how well I knew them didn't matter. With tears streaming down my cheeks, I feared they wouldn't be coming home. Not now. Not ever again.

A soft flare of light drew my attention to the back of the long, dimly lit room. Glancing upward, I realized I had to be on the top floor of the building, in an attic-like space. I briefly wondered what had happened to Posh. I also wondered if she'd been the one to yank me out of the prehistoric room.

Then it hit me. What if I was in another make-believe place? One fashioned after a grisly horror movie like revenge of the pod people or something? Hope surged. Maybe my friends weren't dead after all. Maybe what I was seeing wasn't any more real than the snake monster had been.

But even as I had the thought I knew... real or not... that snake had been extremely dangerous. And if it had killed Brock or me, we'd be just as dead as if we'd been transported back in time to the age of the dinosaurs and met up with a snake as big as my house.

Hot tears slipped down my cheeks. No. My friends were gone. And if my mother and Celeste were there, they were probably gone too.

That thought made my knees buckle and I almost went down. I suddenly couldn't breathe. I'd be all alone in the world. What would I do? Suddenly my life-long disdain for my family's occupation seemed petty and stupid. I'd spent precious years pushing my family away when I should have been embracing them. I'd lost so much time.

And I'd never get it back.

A wave of nausea passed through me. The sickness was so violent it doubled me over and left me retching. What had I done?

The enormity of my mistake took the strength from my legs and they buckled. I hit the floor, my head smacking hard against the gritty wood. The pain was a distant burden, muffled by my misery. At first it didn't occur to me that my reaction was extreme...that my total incapacitation was unequal to the situation. Yes, my family might be gone. But I didn't know that for sure. And if they weren't then curling up into the fetal position on the floor wasn't going to help me get them back.

But the reasonable thoughts bumped up against my misery and I couldn't quite grab hold. The agony was overwhelming. It seeped, thick and dark, through my veins and hardened, denying any other emotion passage.

It was like a living wall of dread, impermeable and hot. A sizzling attack that left behind only pain and destruction. And it smelled of sulfur...

Wait...

Sulfur?

I stirred, trying to concentrate on a thought that was beginning to take shape. Sulfur meant magic. Someone had hexed me. Someone had taken over my will.

I thought of Tabby...of Posh's description of that last time she'd seen her friend. I wondered if she'd experienced something similar.

Pressing my hands against the filthy wood, I tried to push myself off the floor. My muscles were like water and my arms collapsed beneath me. Tears leaked from my eyes but I recognized them for what they were. Proof of my frustration. Somewhere deep inside my mind I knew what was happening to me. But I seemed unable to stop it.

I tried to drag my magic forward. All I managed was a weak fizzle of yellow light. I thought about my cat form but, other than a deep ache in my nailbeds that signaled the start of my claws, nothing happened.

I wanted to rage...to scream...but was unable to do either.

Pain lanced through my skull and I think I cried out. My fingers tightened on the surface of the floor as the pain cut through my brain. My eyes rolled back and I thought I was going to pass out. Nausea blossomed again. My mouth watered but I fought it.

Something danced across my mind. It felt like icy fingertips walking across the tender cells.

I broke into a cold sweat, instinctively fighting the invasion. But the harder I fought it, the more it hurt.

A deep voice said my name and I blinked, twitching from the pain and surprise. Shaking my head, I squeezed my eyes more tightly shut as the fingers danced down my spine. The voice didn't come back, but I had a sense of someone lurking just beyond my awareness.

Suddenly I knew who it was. And I knew what I needed to do.

Gritting my teeth against the pain, I allowed my resistance to fade. My heart pounding with terror, I felt him take hold, his magic wrapping itself around mine.

Heat flared. Healing heat that warmed and strengthened my limbs. Strength returned and I shoved off the floor. Too fast. The world spun as energy whipped through me, spinning silver light in a whirlwind that blocked every other awareness. I forced my eyes open against the dizzying sight and embraced it, opening myself fully to the hungry magic. My claws started to emerge, my fangs to lengthen, and my back arched under the change.

Gritting my teeth, I fought to contain the shift. I wanted my human form, with all its emotional energy to give me power over whatever was stalking me. I pushed to my feet as his voice growled softly through my mind. *Are you okay?*

Yes. I started to run, heading for the spot where I'd seen the flare of light.

Send me a picture of where you are. Mandy and I are on our way.

I did as Deg asked, realizing I'd taken a step I'd later regret. I'd accepted his energy into my core, embraced it in an effort to cast off the oily evil that had taken hold of me.

I felt ten times stronger than I ever had before. And at the same time there was an additional weight to my soul.

Like I was carrying around another human being.

But as the hanging forms around me popped away, one by one, like the mirages they were, I smiled. I might have succumbed to despair at the hand of a truly evil Witch. But the fears that had taken me to my knees were based in reality.

I'd seen the light.

If I could only get my family back, I'd try to be more open to clan business. I'd try to embrace my fate.

After all, I pretty much had to, since I'd let myself

become bonded to the Witch whom, I was truly terrified to realize, was my destiny.

And speaking of said Witch...

A door appeared in front of me and opened as I screeched to a halt, leery of what might come through.

Fortunately for me, the person who stepped through the door was tall, dark-haired and handsome, with worried silver eyes. "Oh thank the gods," Deg said, hurrying toward me. "We were so worried." He pulled me into a hug before I realized what he was going to do. Shock ping-ponged through me as I slammed up against a truly stupendous pair of pecs and a decidedly wash-boardy stomach.

My lungs locked and I forgot to breathe. Then I remembered I was naked and discomfort made me stiffen. Normally shifters are very comfortable in our skin. But I hadn't known the Witch long enough to know if my nakedness would bother or entice.

I wasn't ready to deal with either result.

The door swung wide again and Mandy fixed me with a hostile glare, her gaze moving over us with obvious unhappiness. She handed me a sweatshirt and a pair of jeans and I slipped them on, grateful to her for her thoughtfulness. "Thanks."

Deg stepped away to allow me to dress. I felt his loss like a snap to the solar plexis. I might have even gasped softly as he turned away. "She's okay," Deg told Mandy with obvious relief.

Mandy's glower made it pretty clear she didn't really care. "I see that."

I dropped my hands to my sides and took a long, bracing breath, trying to slow my heartbeat. A soft mewling sound drew my gaze downward. Mable looked up at me, giving me soft eyes, and wound around my ankles. "You brought the kitten into this place?" I quickly scooped her up and buried my face in her sweet-smelling fur.

"Not exactly," Deg told me. When I glanced his way I saw the secret look that passed between them. I didn't like it one bit.

"It's not safe for her here," I told Mandy.

She lifted her hands out to the sides as if she were helpless.

I didn't believe that for a minute.

"She kind of hitchhiked," Deg told me. "I'm not sure exactly how she got here." He frowned at the purring baby in my arms. "Or how she got into this building."

"She's a tricky little devil," Mandy said tightly. "If you ask me, there's more to her than meets the eye."

But I hadn't...asked her. Then I remembered Posh. I grabbed Deg's arm, only a tiny part of my brain taking note of the firm, slightly bulging muscles beneath my fingertips. I quickly dropped my hand so I wouldn't test the delicious firmness like a Summer melon. "I came with a friend. Her name's Posh..." I frowned, realizing she could be in her human form. "Or my mother's receptionist."

Mandy arched a brow. "Her name is *My Mother's Receptionist*?"

I was filled with sudden shame as I realized I still hadn't asked her name. "I don't actually know what her name is. But she was a fa...erm...fluffy cat with multi-colored eyes and strange polka dots in her fur when I last saw her."

Deg's handsome face showed worry again. He and Mandy shared another look. That glance was the last straw for me.

"Okay, tell me what's going on."

Deg shook his head but I didn't give him the chance to lie to me.

"Stop! I saw the looks. Just tell me."

He glanced Mandy's way again and she shrugged. "You might as well tell her."

Deg sighed, stepping closer, and reaching out to squeeze my arm. "It's not good, LA…"

And with those words, the world tilted violently under my feet again. But this time, I wasn't the cause of it.

CHAPTER EIGHTEEN

I stumbled sideways as the floor slanted out from under me. Deg made a grab for my hand but the floorboards swayed violently underneath him and he hit the wall, crashing to the ground.

Mabel's angry yowl filled the air but I couldn't get to her. The floor had shifted again, rolling like ocean waves during a hurricane. I let myself slide to the floor because it was impossible to keep standing. Deg rolled past me, his expression focused and his hands weaving magic upon the air.

I hoped he could come up with something to stop the room from roiling beneath us. Because I was pretty sure I was turning green from all the movement. Horking up my last meal was becoming a real possibility.

I'd never been very good on water. After all, I was as much cat as human wasn't I? Everyone knew how cats felt about water.

A horrendous cracking sound preceded the walls starting to spin. I groaned, sliding across the floor with my hands and feet out to keep from crashing head or shoulder first into anything. Vertigo slapped me hard as the walls spun and the floor rolled. The dizziness made the nausea worse and my muscles turned to mush under the multi-pronged assault.

I cast my gaze hopefully around the room, looking for Deg. I couldn't see him and panic flared. Mandy wasn't rolling around with me either. What if they'd been overcome? Fear for them clashed with fear for myself at the thought. Was I alone in that horror show of a place? Even as my stomach twisted with terror I chastised myself. After all, hadn't I spent my life fighting for independence, declaring I didn't need anybody else's help?

Tears burned my eyes and I angrily shoved them away with one hand. My shoulder slammed against a wooden wave, pain radiating out from the spot and leaving a burning sensation behind. Warm blood ran down my arm as the world continued to pitch and boil.

I finally found Mandy when a particularly violent floorboard wave slammed into me and sent me sprawling to my back. Even as I struggled to find something to anchor to, my gaze slid skyward because...well...I had no choice.

That was when I saw her, hovering above the floor with a wriggling Mabel in her arms.

The kitten was agitated, her sweet gaze fixed on me as I fought to keep from being sent to the bottom of the wooden ocean.

I glowered at the Witch as best I could as I skidded beneath her, barely missing a metal post that, amazingly, stood tall and unmoving amidst the chaos.

She smiled back.

A deep voice called my name. I looked up to find Deg standing on the ceiling, his arm outstretched. "Grab my hand!"

I could barely hear him beneath the thunderous crashing sounds and the spinning walls were making me so dizzy he'd become a blur. But I flung my hand upward, missing his fingers by inches as the middle of the room dropped several feet.

I crashed into the wood-lined sinkhole and hit the bottom, agony shearing through me. I couldn't breathe from the impact and the bones in my back cracked painfully.

I took a beat to draw air into my lungs and then scrambled to my knees and tried to jump from the hole.

Looking up, I realized the walls stretched twelve feet above my head. To make things worse, they were as smooth as glass and I couldn't get a grip.

"LA!" Deg's voice came to me muffled, as if from the end of a long tunnel. I glanced up and responded. "Down here! I can't get out."

"Use your magic," a much higher pitched voice called out. Even when giving me advice to save my life, Mandy's tone was smug and disinterested.

When I reached for the energy within my core, I couldn't find it. Something seemed to be blocking my magic. I envisioned my cat form, with the idea that I might be able to climb the sheer walls if I was wearing a set of nice, sharp claws.

Nothing happened.

"Hang on, LA. I'm coming down," Deg told me. And sure enough, the hole high above my head darkened with his fine form. But even as his fingers danced upon the air, building a shimmering silver web that descended quickly in my direction, I realized there wouldn't be time.

With a sense of horror I recognized that the hole was closing. "Get out, Deg. You'll be trapped!"

His fingers worked feverishly and, to his credit, his magical rescue rope was growing rapidly. I almost thought he might get it done. But the hole was touching his sides and, even from a distance I saw the look of panic on his handsome face as it tightened around him.

"Leave me!" I yelled, tears sliding down my cheeks. Suddenly I couldn't bear the thought of his dying. I barely knew the man, but I knew that his safety was more important than mine. The world needed Deggart Kincaide in it much more than it needed a selfish, self-involved Familiar wearing my name.

The hole squeezed more tightly around Deg, his shoulders contorting under the pressure, but still he wove on.

The rope dangled a couple of feet above me when blood started to stain the walls of the hole around Deg's frantically working form. The bright red blood trickled downward in a vivid stream, a living taunt that because of me someone special would die.

Another someone special.

I screamed his name as the walls began to squeeze me too, splinters of the manic wood piercing me like knives.

"Hang on, LA!" His face was gray, his jaw tight, and I knew it was only a matter of seconds before he was crushed by the deadly magic.

"Dammit, Deg! Leave me!"

But he shook his head. "Jump, LA. Grab the rope."

I realized in that moment we would either live or die together. The thought terrified me because I was pretty sure I was a goner. As the hole above closed, the sides had pinched in just as fast, until I had very little room to move and almost no space to work up to the jump I needed to reach the rope.

But I had to try. Or Deg was going to die trying to save me. I couldn't live with that.

Even if I died too.

I lifted my hands and flexed my thighs, thrusting off my toes with everything I had. I missed the rope by inches. To make things worse, I didn't fall back to the ground. The sides of the hole grabbed hold and held me, feet kicking in desperation, off the ground. I couldn't jump again.

Above me, Deg surrendered a pain-filled scream but I couldn't look up, the wood-lined chasm wedged against my head, holding it at a painful angle and squeezing it like a vise. Agony filled me. Terror made my eyes bulge.

Tears slipped down my face but I didn't even have the air to sob as I died. I was being crushed, ruthlessly, compressed inside a contracting tube of half rotted wood.

The world started to blacken at the edges as my body fought for air that wouldn't come.

The blackness spread, broken only by pinpoints of bright light as my brain died. I felt a final burst of regret for all my mistakes as I started to pass out.

If only I'd done things differently, maybe I wouldn't have died trying to save the people I cared most about in my life…and failed so miserably.

Numbness took away the pain. Resignation sapped me of my fear. The charcoal wash of oblivion called me into its arms and I let it pull me down.

I sank into blessed nothingness, glad to finally be done fighting.

Alas, it wasn't to be.

A bright pair of eyes flashed through my mind. A soft growl scolded me. Guilt found a way into my consciousness. I couldn't just give up. Could I? Too many people were waiting for me to help them.

Deg!

The thought of his death had my fingers stretching upward one last time. With a painful jolt they hit a sizzling pulse of energy. I jerked under its power and silvery light exploded around me, cutting ruthlessly through my delicious oblivion.

I shot out of the hole, my body on fire, and landed screaming and disoriented on the grimy floor of the once roiling room.

I lay there, feeling as if all my limbs had been ripped from their sockets and used to bludgeon me.

I was afraid to open my eyes.

Then something silky and warm rubbed against my arm. Mabel climbed onto my belly and sat there purring, her short tail beating softly against me.

I opened my eyes and groaned.

The room looked perfectly normal. As if nothing had happened.

But I didn't trust it. I pushed slowly and painfully against the floor, managing to get to my knees with a lot of pain-laced groaning.

I scooped the tiny kitten against my chest and kissed the top of her fuzzy head. "I'm glad you're safe."

Then I remembered. *Deg!* My head shot up and I found

him, lying on the floor a few feet away. I scurried over to him. "Deg! Are you okay?"

He groaned too but his eyes fluttered slowly open. "I feel like I've been hit by a truck."

"Me too." I gave him a hand up and we stood there, wobbling a little as we found our sea legs again.

"We need to get out of here," he said, pointing toward a distant door.

I nodded. "Where's Mandy?"

He blinked. We shared a look. And we both looked around.

Deg's eyes darkened with worry as he looked down at the floor.

"I'm sure she didn't get sucked under," I told him. "When I saw her she was floating above it."

His frown deepened. "God forbid she give us a hand."

I chewed my lip. I'd had a similar thought. But then it occurred to me that somebody had to have reversed the evil magic that almost succeeded in killing us. "Maybe she did."

He sighed. "Right. Well, she's always been really good at protecting herself so, I'm guessing she got out of here. Let's go find her."

"And Posh," I said, nodding.

His sexy lips tightened into a thin line. "About that, LA…"

I shook my head. "Let's just get out of here. We can talk after we've saved my family."

CHAPTER NINETEEN

*A*s we ran through seemingly endless hallways, bursting through a boundless array of doors that seemed to lead nowhere at all, I couldn't shake the feeling that the goal I was seeking was very close. Closer than it seemed. The occasional glance at Deg told me he was feeling the same. His handsome face held a perplexed frown and his head swiveled continually, clearly looking for the punchline to the horrendous joke we found ourselves mired in.

I thought of Posh, wondering if she was dead. And Mandy...I suspected it would take more than a floorboard tsunami to kill that Witch. And even Brock. Had the monstrous snake had sexy demon kibble for a midnight snack?

I kept my missing family's fate firmly locked away from my dire thoughts. I couldn't succumb to the deadly collapse of fearing the worst.

There would be time later to mourn them if I discovered they'd shared Tabby's fate.

At the thought, my pulse spiked and something tried to rise up in my memory. Her last words to me, so confusing and seemingly unfocused, suddenly took root in my brain. I jerked to a stop, reaching to grab Deg's wrist as he continued on past.

He dug in his heels and turned, giving me a thoughtful look.

My mind swirled. My head pounded. And memory after seemingly disconnected memory assailed me. I wasn't aware Deg had spoken my name for long moments. It wasn't until he reached out and touched my chin with a warm finger that I snapped out of my reverie.

I blinked up at him. "We're going about this the wrong way."

He frowned. "What do you mean?"

"I mean all magic has become a web now. We've been locked in make-believe inside the web. Fighting our own fears and, unless I miss my guess, our memories of things we've seen or read about. The Witch is using our imaginations against us."

He gave his head a shake, looking around.

We stood in a dank subterranean passageway with dried, black blood staining the walls. The sour stench of burning oil filled the place, thick with the smoke of burning torches jutting from rings embedded in the rock.

I saw the moment Deg recognized the place. "A Cold Grave for Malta."

"What?"

He shook his head, sighing. "This passage. It's right out of a movie I watched as a kid. It terrified me."

I nodded. "I'm pretty sure that giant snake was my doing." I remembered watching a documentary on prehistoric times once. The giant reptiles had kept me on edge for weeks. I was pretty sure I wore my knee-high rubber rain boots everywhere that summer.

"Okay, if we're controlling this…" Deg said.

"Then we should be able to stop it," I finished for him. Glancing around, I felt an eerie calm sliding over me. "Somehow."

"The question is how," he agreed.

"We need to step out of the web," I murmured softly. I looked at Deg. "We need to join our energies and sluff off the imaginary world. Once we can see the web around us we can step out of it."

He nodded, offering me his hand. "Shall we?"

Pulling air into my lungs, I let it out slowly. I stared at his hand for a long moment and then nodded, slipping my fingers through his. Silver sparks shot from our palms, spreading in a sparkling radiance around our joined hands. Deg's energy flowed up my arm and into my core, creating a tightness in my chest that made it hard to breathe. I fought my instinctual resistance, forcing myself to remain open to the seething energy. Gritting my teeth against the effort, I felt my muscles turn to iron and quiver under the strain. As time passed, the effort seemed to ease a bit and, after what felt like a really long time, I released my breath in a slow stream.

The energy totally encompassed us, pulsing and warming me beneath its silvery glow. Deg's sexy silver gaze was locked onto my face, a small smile curving his lips.

I found myself smiling back and, suddenly, it didn't seem so terrible to be joined to the powerful Witch. His expression changed the tiniest bit, morphing into a question.

I nodded, realizing I knew what he was asking me without words.

Then his deep voice eased across my mind. *You ready?*

Yes.

I closed my eyes and sent the energy outward, feeling the moment when it hit the barrier of the false world. It clung there a moment, pushing against the false obstruction for a few beats before, with a firm thought, we rammed through.

There was a small pop in my brain. It hurt only for a second and then warmth oozed past the breech and chaos exploded into my mind's eye.

Multi-colored strands of light flared into view, the strands varying widths and lengths. The fibers were interwoven, the strongest threads like heavy wire...the weakest like the finest filament inside a light bulb. The heavy threads pulsed with vibrant power and, I realized a beat later, seemed to wake to the knowledge that we were there. I suddenly knew what we needed to do. I reached out with my mind and wrapped my magic around the thickest strand.

A high pitched sound pierced my brain and I cried out, my legs buckling beneath me.

Firm hands grabbed me, supporting me until the shrill tone stopped shrieking.

There was a tentative beat of silence.

I felt a warm, treasured presence on the other end of that silence and relief flooded through me. *Mom?*

Another beat of silence followed my hopeful question

and dread filled it. Had it just been wishful thinking to find her there?

LA? You need to run, Peaches. Get out of here. Now!

I was confused. *But you sent for me.*

No. You need to go, LA. I love you, Peaches. I want you to go away and be safe.

I shook my head, even knowing she couldn't see it. *I'm not leaving you behind. Tell me what I need to do.*

Her silence was like a blade to my heart.

Please? I need your help.

A soft, resigned sigh filtered through my consciousness. *First you must see.*

Yeah. I was afraid of that. *How?*

Just, open your eyes, child.

I was terrified to see what I was up against. It seemed as if I'd been chasing the horror for weeks, though I was pretty sure it had been only hours. In that moment I knew I'd found it. And suddenly I didn't want to look.

Deg's hand closed around mine, giving it a supportive squeeze. And I knew I wasn't alone.

I forced my eyes to open.

For one confusing moment I wasn't sure they'd opened. The multi-hued strands of shimmering light still twisted and throbbed before my gaze. I recognized the web and realized I'd seen it once before, in the barrier at *Illusory Park.* Tabby's words came back to me in a rush. *It feeds where we all live...*

"The web!"

I reached out and wrapped my hand around the intertwined strands of magic and screamed as agony speared through me. Twitching against the pain, I was unable to release it once I'd grabbed hold, and felt as if I was being electrocuted where I stood.

Beyond the pain I heard a hundred strident voices, begging me for help. Tears slipped down my cheeks as the power I grasped ripped across my nerves, tearing at the very fabric of the magic that was me.

Hold on, LA! Deg's voice was filled with fear. I clung to that fear because I knew it would lead him to help. A beat later the web in my hand jumped, throwing me to the ground. I skidded across a grimy surface and hit a wall, a warm, hard body slamming into mine.

The web's energy turned manic, flinging us around as Deg and I tried to hold onto it.

The chaos of voices rose with ever increasing urgency, their pleas growing along with the web's frantic behavior.

Then someone screamed...long and filled with anguish...and the web went still in my hand.

I lay there a moment, fearing that if I moved the pain would slice through me again. Everything had gone quiet and the light no longer danced beyond my lids.

I tentatively moved my legs. Then one arm. Keeping my hand wrapped around the throbbing web in my fist, I eased my eyes open. I was looking up at an old metal pipe, rusted and bent, and beyond that, an age-rotted ceiling. Somewhere in the distance water dripped and the stench of filthy wet concrete and decomposing wood made my nose twitch.

I levered myself slowly off the ground and looked around.

It took a moment for me to understand what I was seeing. Once I did, I gave a small cry of horror.

Beside me, Deg groaned softly and pushed upright. He

went completely still as he took in the scene before us. I reached out blindly, groping for his hand. When I found it I slipped my icy fingers into his, squeezing for all I was worth.

The pod people were back. And this time I feared they were real. The multi-colored strands of energy wrapped each cocoon from head to toe, trailing from their bound feet toward the center of the room like strands of demonic Christmas lights.

The energy converged in the center, wrapping around a single figure there.

I gasped as I recognized that figure, my eyes going wide.

"It can't be…"

The figure smiled, its face pale beneath the pulsing aura of the magic strands. "Hello, LA. Strange seeing you here."

I shook my head and stood, still gripping the latent web of magic the Witch had used to contain us. "Why?"

The figure shrugged, dark gaze widening with pleasure. "Because I could."

Deg stood too and I could feel his confusion. "But he was…"

"Dead," I finished for him. "Yes. He was dead."

Jacob Withers cocked his head, fixing me with a pitying look. "It's a shame you've forced yourself into my lair, LA." Then he smiled. "But I'm really glad you did. You and your Witch were the last pieces I needed to complete my web. Now that you're here…" Oily black energy shot out of his magic cocoon and snagged me, spinning so quickly I was halfway encased in its cold power before I realized what had happened.

Deg gave a throaty cry and I watched him shoot skyward, struggling against the twining black magic as it bound him from shoulder to knees.

As soon as the oily magic touched my skin I felt its taint draining my will. I fought desperately, even when my mind told me it would be so much easier to stop. There was no way I was going to let him steal my life, Deg's life, and the lives of my family and friends just because he could.

He'd have to go through me first.

Use the web, Deg's husky, strained voice grated across my mind. *It's connected to him.*

My scattered thoughts struggled for a moment to figure out what he was telling me. But a warm throbbing in the energy web I still clutched in one hand finally broke through my fogginess and I tightened my fingers on the thing. Far from being dead, as I'd believed before, the web had just gone quiet for a moment. It was coming back to life in my hand, pulsing and flaring with light, and I realized it would soon pull me into its force, locking me down and sucking me dry as it had done the others in the room.

I couldn't let that happen. If the demon at the center of the *Familiar, Inc.* takeover planned to use the web to pull energy away from Deg and me, I wondered what he would do if we gave him a bit of his own medicine.

Can you help? I asked Deg, even as I sent tentative threads into the web in my hand, exploring...searching out its faults.

Yes. He grated out. If I could turn my head I was pretty sure I'd find Deg struggling mightily. He sounded as if he were using everything he had just to stay alert and fight off the irresistible pull of Jacob's oily magic.

"It's really fortuitous for me, LA, that you finally succumbed to your place in the world," Jacob said in his arrogant, slightly nasal tone. I'd always hated that arrogance when we'd been an item, and had always wondered what formed the basis of it. Clearly he thought a lot of himself.

But hadn't he proven he was justified? Not many magical creatures could have done what he'd accomplished. No Familiar should be able. Even a Witch would struggle to accomplish it. Yet he'd managed to imprison an entire, powerful group for his own use. It was irritatingly impressive and it made me cranky. "At least I understand my place, Jacob," I told him as I sent questing fingers of energy into the magic grid in my fist. I felt the aura of Deg's magic too, just a faint shadow that I hoped Jacob wouldn't notice. "*You* seem to have overstepped your bounds."

If it was possible, his laughter was even more snotty than his voice. "Really, LA? I've made the most powerful Familiars my bitch. Do you really think I've gone beyond my abilities?"

I shrugged, my mind fighting off the growing allure to give in…to just let him pull me under his influence. I was so tired. So frustrated by his ability to continually stay one or two steps ahead.

"I would have never been able to snag Deggart the elusive without your bond, LA," he continued. "For that you have my eternal gratitude. Maybe I'll even let you have some autonomy as a reward."

I frowned. What did he mean? Why did he call Deg

elusive? Doing a mental head shake, I tightened my fingers around the network in my fist and sent a testing jolt of energy into it, carefully tugging on the thinnest strand I could find. I hoped the weakness of the thread would allow me to avoid his notice. "Don't count your kitties before they're born, Jacob. You're right, you have managed to *temporarily* capture some of our best. But you won't be able to hold onto all this power for long. We'll be back."

He stared at me, his smug smile widening with confidence. "You think so? Maybe you don't understand what I've done."

The micro-thin strand slipped from the web with a tiny surge, its energy shimmering through my fingertips and sliding into my system. I held my breath that Jacob hadn't felt it and my heart skipped a beat when he cocked his head, thinking he was going to react.

But he only nodded. "I suppose it would be too much to ask for anyone to understand at this juncture, but you will. You'll all understand some day. I'll have to satisfy myself with that."

Another strand slipped free of the grid, its light going dark as the energy it had contained slid into Deg.

My system thrummed with frustration. We had to step up the process or we'd be toast long before we made a difference. With a stab of horror, I realized we'd have to capture a much larger strand. But once we'd done that we'd be out of time. We'd have to move fast because Jacob would be on us.

I'm going for my grandmother's strand, I told Deg. *You grasp Mom's.*

With the two most powerful strands in our grasp, we should have enough energy to turn the tables on Jacob.

At least I hoped we would.

Deg's thoughts were chaotic. He didn't respond and I risked a glance in his direction. I gasped. His large frame was almost entirely covered in multi-hued strands. He was nearly gone.

Jacob's hateful laugh made me snap my attention back to him. "You see, LA, I have already pulled your boyfriend into my network. I'd have you too if I wanted."

I sneered at him, so angry and scared I was shaking with it. "Then why haven't you? There's no reason to keep me alive, is there? You're within a hair of getting everything you want, Jacob. Everything there is. But then what? Who will know what you've done? Who will there be to appreciate the feat? You'll be all alone. All that power and no place to go."

His smile finally dimmed. I'd chosen my words carefully, built on the knowledge of the man I'd dated for almost a year. He was a vain man. A selfish, greedy man. But he had always craved the limelight. He'd always fought to prove he was better than everyone else. It was that competitive hunger that had finally succeeded in breaking us up. He hadn't been able to stand the idea that I might be as powerful as he was. Or maybe even more powerful.

At first he'd tried to wriggle his way into the Familiar hierarchy, sucking up to my family in an attempt to rise in the ranks. But when he finally realized he'd never be anything but an employee, and one who was outside the circles of power, he'd begun to resent me because I had a natural spot within the power circle. One that I didn't even want.

"The magical world doesn't stop with *Familiar, Inc.*, LA."

I shook my head, my fingers of energy sifting through the web looking for my grandmama's strand. If I could only grasp one, it had to be the strongest. I had no idea if it would be enough. But I knew that if it wasn't we were all lost. "No. But you know how tribal the magic world is, Jacob. You're a Familiar, a Witch's demonic helper, that's all you'll ever be to the others. No matter how much power you have, you'll be seen as an outsider. You'll be less. Unwanted and never trusted."

His dark gaze flared with hate, his lips thinning. "I'll make them accept me. I'll strike them down until they do."

I forced my lips to curve. "That's a great plan, Jacob. They'll love you for that."

He stiffened, his body shaking violently under a terrible emotion. I recognized the condition. He was overloaded with power. Magical adrenaline. His system was saturated, bloated with energy. With all the magic he was holding, it was probably a struggle just to maintain equilibrium. I tensed as his eyes rolled back in his head, his hands coming up, fingers spreading, and electricity arcing between them. He was a hair away from going nuclear. And I feared he'd blow the whole place apart if he did.

I needed to move fast. I grasped Celeste's strand and yanked, ripping it from the web. It sizzled in my hand, burning my flesh and dancing violently as I tried to control the rabid magic contained there. I could barely hold onto it. But I was afraid if I released the strand it might snap back into place in the network. I couldn't allow that to happen. The surge would definitely send Jacob into orbit and I feared he'd take everyone tied to him along on the deadly ride.

Within seconds the manic strand was going to escape my grasp. I needed to let Grandmamma know it was me. If we could only work together...

A horrible shriek filled the air. A flash wave of magic scoured the room, turning the atmosphere toxic with flame and oily magic.

My lungs felt scorched with every breath and the agony of breathing the toxic air made me fear they were actually on fire under my ribs. I was out of time. Making a sudden decision, I lowered my resistance and allowed my energy to slide into the strand I held in my hand.

It jumped, violently repelling the invasion, and flared into pinkish white light before clamping down on my energy and ripping it away from me.

Agony speared through me, tearing at the cells in every part of my body, and the floor came up to meet me with a horrible crunching sound.

All I could do was lay there, writhing and twitching, as my magic was ripped violently away.

CHAPTER TWENTY

*I*t's me, I whispered desperately in my mind. *Stop tearing at me.* I was absurdly unhappy with the weakness of my own internal communication. But the pain and sense of violent intrusion made it nearly impossible to think, let alone talk coherently.

The ripping pain continued unabated, so I tried again.

Celeste!

The ferocity of her response dipped, hesitated, and then started to ease. *LA, is that you, child?* Her voice sounded scratchy, as if from interference or pain.

I thought about nodding, even tried to get my neck muscles to cooperate, and then realized she couldn't see it. Licking painfully dry lips, I said, *Yes. I came to get you out.*

Grandmama's easy chuckle filtered through our tenuous connection. *Child, you never did have a lick of sense...*

I sighed. *Can we not do this now, Celeste?*

Your mother has always taken up for you...made excuses... but you're eternally capricious and undependable.

My temper flared. *I'm here now, aren't I? I don't see anybody else trying to help.* Guilt stabbed as I realized my words weren't strictly true. My friends had tried to help too. They'd accompanied me in our failed attempt, endangering themselves. If they were in peril...or worse...it was all my fault. I'd brought them into the mess we found ourselves in and I'd insisted on moving forward even through life-threatening events designed to stop us. *My friends and I followed Jacob's trail...*

Jacob? Celeste questioned. *What does he have to do with this?*

Was it possible she didn't know? *This is all his doing, Grandmama. He's the one behind the explosion at Familiar, Inc. He killed Tabby and kidnapped you and mother. If Posh hadn't come to me we'd never have found you. And now I can't find her and I'm worried.*

I could feel Celeste's confusion in my mind. It made me distinctly uncomfortable. She'd always been so sharp and intuitive...twelve steps beyond everyone else. I hated to see what Jacob had done to her. For that alone I was going to make sure he got his due.

LA...

Her voice was filled with censure. I could see a lecture about succumbing to emotion coming. The Queen didn't cotton to emotional displays or judgements. According to the Queen of the Familiars, every decision must be based on logic and fact...measured against the common good. No individual Witch, Demon or Familiar was worth endangering the rest. Suddenly I feared she was going to tell me to go away...to leave them and rebuild the company she and my mother had worked so hard to build. I couldn't do that. I wouldn't! *Grandmama! Just listen to me. We don't have much time. Jacob is draining you all of your magic. Deg and I need to turn the tables on him. We need your energy so we can use it against him.*

I sensed her resistance and prepared myself to argue my case...fortunately it wasn't necessary.

Your mother and I came up with the same plan. We've been working on combining our energies since he brought us here.

But aren't you afraid he'll feel what you're doing?

How could he?

He holds you captive...

Don't be silly, child. Well, technically that's true. We unfortunately allowed ourselves to be hexed into an incapacitated state while we were dazed from the attack. But no one has captured our energy. We've managed to repel every attempt so far.

Relief flooded me. *Thank the gods!*

Yes, but it won't do us a lot of good unless we can figure out a way to fight back.

Tell me what I can do.

I sensed her hesitation. *What's wrong?* I asked.

I'm afraid of what will happen to the others, she admitted softly. A sense almost of shame filled her admission. *They're tied to the core now. If we overcome the system it might kill them.*

My world wobbled a bit as I realized my grandmama was just as susceptible to emotion as I was. Though I'd always hated her cold calculations, I'd nurtured a certain respect for her that she was able to rise above the weakness inherent in sentimental thought. I swallowed hard, knowing what I needed to do. *We need to trust that they will find a way to survive, Celeste. We have no choice. Our world needs you and Mom in it. We'd be lost without you. And frankly, if we don't do this everyone will die anyway.* I was horrified as I said the words. They felt so cynical and cold. But even so, I knew it was the truth.

And I could feel that Celeste knew it too.

She sighed softly. *I'm proud of you, LA.*

I resisted the gratification trying to rise up at her words. I felt ugly inside...hateful. I worried that my detached reasoning was based only on the fact that I wanted my family back. Could I be that selfish? I didn't know. But I knew it didn't matter. We needed to stop Jacob.

Tell me what you need me to do. I repeated, tossing guilt away.

The problem is twofold. So far your mother and I haven't figured out how to attack both levels. Against the combined power of all of our kind, we need every bit of our joined energy to defeat the Demon. You and your friends must destroy its barriers. As soon as they're down we'll attack.

Consider it done, I told her with more confidence than I felt.

Not so fast, child. What I'm asking you to do is extremely dangerous. The barrier is as much a protection for us as it is for the Demon. Once you break it down you'll be in danger of being sucked in, pulled into the energy vortex that's keeping the protections alive. You must anchor yourself somehow to this world.

I thought of that for a moment and then nodded. *I think I have a way.* My tone was filled with confidence I didn't feel.

May the gods go with you, child.

And with you, Grandmama.

I felt our connection slide away and knew that she would keep a wall between us until Jacob was defeated. It was the only way. We couldn't risk him sensing her when I attacked. And she couldn't risk dragging me into the line of fire when she and my mom took him down.

I pushed those thoughts away and reached for Deg in my mind. He was a tiny flicker of light at the very center of my core. Small and weak, but still pulsing. I fed some of the magic I'd borrowed from Celeste into him and waited for him to strengthen.

Panic flared in my breast as the tiny light representing the last of his energy flashed once, a tiny silver flare, and then died completely out.

Deg! I screamed, fear making my energy stutter as I tried again to feed him what I'd gained.

Static danced across my mind, Deg's voice weak and thready against the sound. *Go...*

I wasn't sure I'd heard him right. Was he telling me he had to leave? Did he mean in a permanent sense? I opened my eyes and looked at him, despair making it hard to breathe. He was fully covered with pulsating colored strands, his long body wrapped tightly, cocooned like the rest. I shook my head, one hand reaching in his direction. *Deg! I need your help. You have to stay with me.*

Nothing. Tears burned the backs of my lids. I was on my own.

Frantically, I reached out to Mandy, looking for the remembered spark of her fire-red aura. I didn't see it in my mind. Disappointing as that was, it wasn't a surprise. I had no connection to the Witch, except through Deg and as far as I knew they'd never meshed magics.

Still, I'd seen enough of her capabilities to know that she shouldn't be easy for Jacob to take down. I did a mental head shake. No. Mandy couldn't be cocooned with the others.

Could she?

Though everything inside me railed against it, I did a quick scan of the dark pods hanging from the high ceiling and saw no telltale pulse of red.

Earth to LA? Have I lost you already?

Jacob's hated voice made the hairs on my arms stand at attention. He seemed perfectly unconcerned with the idea that I might defeat him. That realization made me mad. And terrified that he was right. But most of all it made me determined to prove him wrong. *I was just thinking how much fun it will be to kick your multi-hued butt.*

He chuckled darkly. *That's going to be hard to do in your current state, don't you think?*

I glanced down at myself. Or at least I tried. My head wouldn't move. I rolled my gaze downward and saw the crisscrossing play of lighted strands around my body. Like Deg I was almost fully engulfed. I fought anxiety. It was okay. He might have bound my body but he hadn't bound my energy. Understanding hit me. Deg was okay! His magic was most likely still intact like mine. It was just that Jacob had muffled it somehow. Made it impossible for me to see. He probably couldn't see mine either. Which meant... I flicked Deg another look, finding his silvery gaze locked on mine. There was a question in his eyes, one that I couldn't answer verbally or even through our mental pathways. But I could send him a sign. One he couldn't possibly miss.

I held his gaze and concentrated on the core of my

magic, pulling it forward as far as it would go under Jacob's oily warding.

The roiling energy sat just beneath my skin, pulsing with latent power, hungry for release. I held it there, letting it build until it burned me with its intensity. I'd only have one chance and I didn't want to blow it. I didn't know how the connection between Deg and I worked. We hadn't had time to discuss or practice its use. But I trusted that it gave me more energy than I would otherwise have. I was going to need every bit of it.

Still holding Deg's gaze, I gritted my teeth against the agony of holding back my magic and then, slowly blinking once, twice, and then a third time, I lowered my shields and let the magic fly.

CHAPTER TWENTY-ONE

*S*ilvery orange fireworks exploded into the dark space, painting it with a riot of flashing illumination. The magic roared from my pores, burning me as it went, and washed, unfocused and violent through the room.

The tangle of strands around my body tightened, constricting my chest and making it hard to breathe, but I forced myself to ignore it, pinning all my attention on the hated form of the man at the center of the nightmare.

Jacob's eyes went wide, his mouth opened as if he would speak, and then the energy Deg and I released hit him, blowing him back several steps to smash up against a filthy brick wall. His dark hair flew away from his head, creating a wildly gyrating aura around his pale face, like a male Medusa with snakes for hair.

I gritted my teeth as the strands tightened further around me. Pain slashed across my limbs as the bright energy sliced through my skin and it was all I could do to keep my feet. But the energy I carried wasn't abating, if anything I thought it had grown stronger as the strands bit into me.

Jacob's form narrowed, rounded in strange curves, and his hair lengthened into longer dark gold snakes. A different pair of eyes widened as the first strand unraveled and snapped away into the darkness. A curvy pair of lips thinned with pique as three more strands sprang away.

Deg's body surged upright, lifting off the ground and dancing helplessly at the end of his entanglements. I barely had time to realize what I'd seen before my body too flew upward, the violence of the movement sending me clear to the ceiling and smacking me hard against it. The impact stunned me, made me lose focus for a beat, and the energy I'd been channeling blipped away.

The figure in the center of the chaos swelled, head falling back and chest inflating as if it were taking a deep breath.

I knew I had to act quickly or the Demon would recover enough to defeat us. Even as I had the thought, the creature lifted its arms and, eyes flaring with fire, threw an oily blanket of black energy against our remaining magic. The sulfurous power hit our magic and spread, snuffing it out wherever it touched.

LA! Deg's voice was filled with command, reverberating through my brain, and I reacted instantly. I pulled myself off the floor, throwing out my hands and sending several more of the constrictive magic strands sizzling away from me.

I expanded my chest with a relieved breath and focused my gaze on the demonic figure at the center of the morass. My heart broke as I realized how fully I'd been fooled. But I shoved those feelings aside and reached for Deg, wrapping spitting fingers of energy around the core of his energy and yanking it into my sphere.

I felt him swell as his energy fused with mine. The Demon's oily power throbbed, gaining another inch in sheer desperation, and then started to retreat as we threw everything we had against it.

Several more strands popped away, snaking eagerly back toward their owners, and the Demon threw back its head and shrieked, the sound inhuman and painful to my unprotected ears.

The black wall of energy retreated and Deg and I moved closer as it went. That was the first time I realized we were no longer contained by strands. Only a couple, very thin strands from weak or young familiars still clung to us. I sent magic into those strands to keep them strong until we could carefully extract them.

The Demon writhed at the center of our storm. I finally saw the secondary attack that had no doubt been being waged from the start. Two strands of magic, reddish orange and as thick as my arm, assaulted the thing without mercy as we tugged chunks of its barrier magic away and approached.

It fell to its knees, arms finally dropping to brace it on the floor, and collapsed onto itself, face on the floor covered in a thick blanket of dark gold hair.

Weariness finally hit me. My knees wobbled and I stopped, retracting my magic as the creature on the floor jerked, arched its back, and returned to a form that it most likely hoped would tug on my heartstrings.

Posh shivered once and dropped to her haunches,

lifting her strange-colored eyes to my face. *You don't want to do this, cher.*

She was right. I didn't. *I thought you were one of the good ones*, I told her sadly.

She shook her head, lifting a paw to lick as if she hadn't a care in the world. *I am. I only wanted to prove to the magical world that Familiars are strong and worthy opponents. I figured you'd thank me for that, given your own feelings on the matter.*

Guilt turned to bile in my throat. I swallowed hard to dispel it. "Have I ever done anything to make you think I sanctioned raping everybody of their power?" Even as I asked the question I feared her answer. Had I?

Have you ever shown you cared about the others? Even one little bit?

My heart stuttered as I realized she was right. I shook my head, trying to deny her words to myself.

I was going to let everyone go unharmed. You have my word on that.

Unbidden, a picture of poor Tabitha flashed through my mind. *Tabby would beg to differ*, I said.

Her paw dropped back to the floor and her gaze found mine again. *She was going to expose me. Surely you can understand why I couldn't let her do that?*

Deg came up beside me and my magic rose to the surface as if to greet him. The change created a weird shifting sensation in my chest that had me struggling to breathe. It would take me a while to get used to that. I looked up at him and he gave me a pitying look. He dropped an arm around my shoulders and pulled me close in silent understanding.

The darkness shifted and Mandy sauntered out, my

mother and Celeste on her heels. One by one the pods behind them were unraveling, leaving only two very small pods hanging from the rafters.

No. I was wrong. Tears burned my eyes as I spotted the blackened husk of one pod, curled on the floor and unmoving.

Posh's treachery had claimed another victim.

I forced my emotions back. We still had work to do. "We need to help these children," I told Deg.

He nodded. "Maybe if we feed energy into them as we pull the dark magic away?"

The shadows near the floor shifted and a tiny form padded toward us, tail curling lazily behind her. I smiled at the kitten.

Mabel gave me a happy meow but stopped, dropping to her haunches and throwing Posh a wary look.

The oversized cat returned the favor, her body language clearly telegraphing her dislike of the kitten. *Get lost stupid cat.*

Mabel cocked her head, her lips turning upward in what looked for all the world like a smile. *Make me*, she said in her childish voice. I frowned, worried that she would taunt such a powerful Demon. *Mabel, you shouldn't...* Before I could finish, Posh rose up on her hind legs, one thick paw shooting straight out and sending black energy zinging through the air.

I flexed to throw myself at the kitten, knowing even as I did that I wouldn't be fast enough to save her, but was astounded when Posh's magic lifted into the air, slamming toward the shadows, where the two remaining pods swung lazily below the rafters.

The oily energy encircled the small pods, yanking

them into a tight embrace that strained the strings holding them off the ground.

The big cat yowled angrily, flinging herself into the air and twisting around to land on her feet near the door. *Let me leave and I won't kill them.*

I blinked, horrified. For a long moment we all stilled, faces clearly showing our horror. Then I swallowed and lifted my hands. "Let them go."

The cat wavered, twisted and arched, bones cracking loudly as she transformed in the blink of an eye into the receptionist whose name I didn't know. Self-loathing took a chunk out of me before I smacked it down. There'd be time later to kick myself for being an insensitive clod.

There were bigger concerns in that moment.

"Please don't hurt them," I pleaded.

A slightly hunched form stepped out of the shadows, hands outstretched in supplication. The woman's face was white as a sheet and tears painted tracks over the chalky skin. She was horribly thin, with dark purple arcs beneath eyes that had once been beautiful. I gasped softly when I realized it was Holly. My gaze slid to the smaller pods, which had to contain Lena and Kristopher, Fresh horror twisted my belly. "Take me," Holly told the Demon holding the children captive. "Please leave my children be."

Posh...because it was the only name I had to go by... smiled meanly. "I don't think so."

My mother stepped into the light, her beautiful face nearly as thin and white as the mother's. Her appearance made me gasp softly with shock. Anger for her treat-ment...for all their treatment...flooded me.

"Let them go, Star. This is beneath even you."

I felt my mouth turn up in a sneer at the woman's name. She was about as close to star-like as the giant snake had been.

"Let me leave safely and I'll release them."

The mother inched toward her children. I had an inkling she thought to try to save them if the evil Star sent death their way.

"You won't get far," Celeste said.

There was movement behind my mother and a skeletal hand reached out of the shadows and landed heavily on her shoulder. I gasped aloud as my grandmama came into the light.

She'd aged thirty years.

Tears flowed down my cheeks. Familiars aged very slowly and she'd held her youthful beauty much longer than most because of her extraordinary power. Vanity might be a weakness, but Celeste had always embraced it. She'd been so proud of her looks. It would kill her to know how she looked after succumbing to the Demon's foul magic. But even worse, she was bent and frail. The beautiful strawberry blond hair looked like a wig sitting on an emaciated old woman's head.

I lifted my hand and jammed my fist into my mouth to keep from crying out.

Rage tore magic from my core and, before I knew what I was doing, I'd freed it, allowing it to spit and flare around me. "Release those children, Demon." To my shock, my voice had deepened and grown, filling up the enormous attic space and slamming against the walls.

Star's eyes widened slightly but then she smiled. I knew in that moment what she was going to do.

I couldn't let her kill the children.

But there was only one thing that would stop her.

LA, look past the Demon. Deg's voice was soft but insistent, burrowing into my rage and forcing me to hear. My eyes found the door behind her and saw it open a crack. A slim figure with dark hair snuck through and my eyes met Mandy's. She held my gaze a beat and then nodded.

I understood as though she'd spoken.

The kids, I told Deg as I sprang.

With an enraged yowl, Star sent her deadly energy along the strands. It surged along the magic fibers like fire along a fuse, emitting a black, sulfurous stench into the air as it went. I ran directly for it as Deg and my mother leapt toward the children.

A pain-filled scream drenched the air. The air boomed once and everyone else hit the ground, covering their ears as energy sliced through the atmosphere in wide, deadly blades, cutting away huge chunks of wood and ripping away the ceiling. Fire burned everywhere it touched, smoke billowed. I barely noticed any of it as I reached for the children's life strands, my gaze locked on the rapidly approaching black energy.

I flung myself into the air and grabbed the fibers as I fell. I hit and rolled, wrapping my other hand around the burning threads and sending my own energy into it in an attempt to shut it down.

Posh's magic hit mine and burrowed through as if it didn't even exist. Deg was suddenly there, wrapping his big hands around the threads ahead of mine. They thrummed under the levels of power we sent into them, flame roared from beneath his palms and mine.

I thought for a moment that it wouldn't be enough.

Despite our combined efforts, Posh's black energy burned through our grips, forcing us to continually back away to try to get in front of it.

Holly's soft sobbing just about did me in. The sound of her cries told me we were running out of time and the children would be the ones who paid for our failure.

I gritted my teeth and forced more energy into the already bloated strands. They began to splinter and a new fear joined all the others. What if we burst the energy strands before we beat Posh back? Would the children die?

I didn't have the answer to that. All I had was hope and determination.

Giving off another primal scream, I gritted my teeth and dragged at the remaining core of my magic, sending it into the strands between my fingers and praying it would be enough.

Finally, in minute increments, the progress of Posh's hated magic began to slow. I held on even as my energy started to falter, praying I'd have enough to see it through.

The last of Posh's magic halted beneath our hands, spitting angrily between our fingers. We were almost there. But I wouldn't relax until we'd severed the thread that gave the Demon access to the kids. Unfortunately, I was afraid it would also harm the children.

I looked up, heart pounding with fear. My mother and Celeste were bent over the kids, frantically removing strands of Star's magic. Unfortunately, each strand had to be carefully extracted or the children would die.

I could feel the tiny pulse of their life force beneath my fingertips. And I was terrified when I felt it start to wane.

"They're dying!" I screamed, aching to release the strand and help.

Celeste just shook her head and kept working. Steady and slow.

Deg and I shared a look and I saw my fear mirrored in his gaze. Then he smiled…a soft smile that made my pulse slow and my terror ease.

They'll be okay, LA.

I shook my head. He couldn't possibly know that. But his words somehow made me feel better anyway. And my magic rose in answer to his energy, throbbing again at my core.

I felt something pressing against my shin and looked down. Mabel wound herself through my arms and beneath the strands. I lifted them quickly. "Be careful, kitten!"

But she raised up on her haunches and bumped her soft head against mine, sliding it off and along the spitting strand. I gave an alarmed cry just as the strand went dark and the energy sifted away.

A roaring sound erupted behind me. I turned to find the floor opening up into another chasm and Mandy and Star engaged in a deadly battle on the razor edge of the opening. Mandy had built a quelling web and was trying to wrap it around Star, but the Demon was too quick and kept sidestepping the net, only to send massive bolts of energy slamming into Mandy every time she escaped.

A plume of fire burst from the bowels of the open floor and a sulfurous stench filled the room in a gray cloud. I could barely breathe under the horrendous reek. Coughing erupted around me and I knew that if anyone had any energy left after being drained by Star for several days, the smoke and heat of the growing hell-fire would rob them of it.

"Get out of here!" I yelled and then took off toward Mandy and Star. A big hand grasped my arm, dragging me to a halt before I'd gone very far. I glared over my shoulder at Deg. "Let me go, Witch!"

He shook his head, sliding his grip down to grasp my hand. "Together we're stronger."

I frowned, unhappy, but realized he was right. "Let's blast this bitch."

His handsome face curved into a knee-melting smile and he nodded. Then we turned toward the battling duo and, catching Mandy's eye, sent her scurrying for cover.

Thinking she'd won the battle, Star swung around and laughed. She lifted her hands into the air, prepared to send more evil into the room, and then stopped when she spotted Deg and me.

We stood in an aura of sizzling energy that was three times our width and reached all the way to the ceiling. It danced around us, hungry for the taste of Demon magic.

Our hands hung down at our sides, fingers dancing softly as we created death for the evil creature standing across from us.

Fire spat upward, forming a toxic barrier that Star no doubt thought would work in her favor.

But she didn't know what we could accomplish together.

Or did she?

Her eyes widened. Her stance stiffened. And she glanced quickly toward the door behind her.

She wouldn't make it.

Deg and I closed our eyes, pictured the Demon's demise, and threw up our hands to send a wave of deadly energy in an inescapable wash to slam against Star. It wrapped around her like huge, spitting fingers of fire and lifted her off the ground. Carrying her out over the mouth of the hell-fire pit, it shot downward, dragging her straight to Hell.

The pit closed with an elongated popping noise and the room went completely quiet.

It was if everyone in the room heaved a collective sigh of relief. I turned toward Celeste, half afraid to find out how the children were. My mouth dry, my stomach tight with dread, I peered past my family and saw...

Relief soared.

The two small Familiars were sitting up, sans magical restraints, smiling and talking to their very relieved mother who had wrapped herself around them like a Winter coat and was shedding tears of relief.

Deg dropped an arm around my shoulders. "We did it."

I turned my gaze upward, favoring him with a weary smile. "We did. Thanks so much for joining the battle. I know it wasn't your fight."

He shook his head, opening his mouth to respond. But the words never made it past his lips.

The door in front of us burst open and slammed back against the wall with an explosive bang. All eyes turned to the Demon standing there, eyes wild and hair standing straight up on his head.

Tension shot upward and energy spat from a dozen fingerprints, ready to do battle again.

Brock frowned, scrubbing a filthy hand over his sexy,

square jaw. He looked terrible. But he was alive. "Did I miss all the fun?"

Deg walked over and slapped him on the back, grimacing at the wet splat as his hand connected with Brock's sodden shirt. "It looks like you were right in the middle of it." He pulled his hand away and something slimy oozed toward the ground. "What in the world happened?"

Brock shook his head. "It's a really long story. I'll just sum it up by telling you that the inside of a massive snake is not a nice place to be."

"Erg," I said, recoiling. "Are you all right?"

He got a cocky smile. "Of course. Well…" He rubbed one shoulder and I noticed the bright spot of fresh blood there, probably from a fang. "I'm better than the snake anyway."

I looked down as a tiny, soft form wrapped itself warmly around my ankle. "Hey, girlfriend." Mabel narrowed her gaze softly and meowed as I greeted her. Reaching down, I lifted the kitten off the floor and snuggled her up under my chin.

"There's something slightly off about that cat."

My head shot up as Mandy limped slowly in my direction, her pretty face fixed into a frown. "She's just a sweet kitten," I objected.

Mandy didn't argue, but she fixed a speculative gaze on the baby cat, her eyes narrowing thoughtfully.

"I'm so proud of you, LeeAnn," a loving voice said from behind. I turned to my mother and allowed a warm bloom of happiness to fill my belly. Everyone was safe. My coldly assessing decision seemed to have turned out okay. It was safe to feel good about making my family proud.

But I hoped I'd never have to play Russian Roulette with anyone's lives again.

That was why I preferred to leave the leadership roles to my mother and Celeste.

"Thanks, Mom."

She gave me a quick hug, laughing softly when Mabel gave a soft yip of complaint from being squashed between us. Mother rubbed the tip of a finger beneath Mabel's soft chin and the kitten was soon purring happily.

"How did you find us?" Celeste asked.

I turned to her, barely containing my frown. Celeste looked so frail, so much older than she had before she was captured. The entire thing seemed to have taken too much out of her. I shot my mother a quick look and saw her gaze fill with sadness. But she forced a smile and turned to Grandmama. "She's a tracker, Mama."

I shook my head. "I wish I could take credit for this. Unfortunately, Posh brought me here." The full realization of how I'd been tricked hit me then, washing out any pride I might have felt at defeating the demon. "She fooled me completely."

Grandmama patted my shoulder. "Don't feel bad, child. Star fooled all of us."

"She's always been very unobtrusive...non-descript." Mother shrugged. "I didn't pay attention and that was apparently what she wanted. I now realize she had to have been masking herself somehow. I should have known she was up to something."

"I barely noticed her," I agreed guiltily. "I didn't even know her name."

"I didn't either."

I glanced around to the young mother, firmly holding the hands of her two children as she approached.

Holly gave me a soft smile. "Thank you so much for saving my kids. I owe you one."

Shaking my head, I returned the smile. "You don't owe me anything." The sting of guilt coursed through me again. My decision to go after Star could have just as easily killed her children. "I just got lucky."

"I'm not buying that." Her smile wavered as she glanced toward the still-smoking spot where Star had disappeared. "I walked past her nearly every day and barely acknowledged her existence. I wonder if that's why she did what she did."

"Possibly," my mother said, giving the woman a squeeze. "But that's on her. Not us. She could have done a hundred things to bring herself out of the shadows. Good things to help the world. Instead she chose to embrace her demonic side and cause harm. That isn't on you or me or anybody else. The responsibility for that decision is completely on her."

In that moment I realized why my mother was almost as good a leader as Celeste. She was right. And she'd boiled the whole thing down to a correct, if coldly factual, accounting that placed blame where it belonged. "How was she able to manage all this without anyone knowing how powerful she was?" I asked.

"I'm going to look into that," Grandmama said on a frown. "I believe Star had some powerful magic in her family, but we'd given up on her ever reaching that potential since she never showed signs of being anything but average."

"The Ley lines didn't hurt either," my mom offered. "She was able to tap into them and enhance her powers several fold."

"Terrifying," Deg said, shaking his dark head.

Celeste nodded. "Now we move forward. We heal, rebuild and grow stronger." Her smile softened into weariness. "Starting tomorrow. Right now, after we tend to immediate business, I think I could use a few hours rest."

We all looked toward the back corner of the smoky room, where a burly male Familiar whose name was Tom if I remembered correctly, bent down and gently pulled Star's second victim off the floor. We watched sadly as he carried the gray haired woman out of the room. "We need to let Francie's family know what happened to her," Mom told Celeste, wrapping an arm around Grandmama's frail shoulders. "And then we can go home."

Celeste nodded.

I watched them walk toward the door, followed by all the Familiars Star had held hostage in that terrible place. I knew I should feel happier, but there was a hole in my chest that I wasn't sure how to repair.

"A penny for your thoughts?" Deg asked from just behind me. I turned, shaking my head. "I'm just really tired I guess."

He held my gaze a long moment. "You do look tired. But that's not what's bothering you."

Irritation bloomed. The last thing I needed or wanted at that moment was to have someone force me to face my fears. "It'll wait."

We walked a few steps and then I remembered. "Hey, you never told me how you found me here?"

"Simple really. I was able to get us close by reading the energy we bound up in the rug at your house. Then Mandy tracked you here and we realized you'd gone on without us." He frowned.

"I'm really sorry. Posh came to me and offered to show me and only me where the Demon was." I shrugged. "I didn't think I could refuse her offer."

He shook his head. "I know you're used to doing things by yourself..."

"But now you think I should ask you for permission before I do anything." I glared up at him and saw in the darkening of his silver gaze when his anger rose to meet mine.

"Not at all, LA. I'm not your master and you're not my servant. You're thinking like the old ways. Things are different now. We can be partners, but it will take some effort to figure out how to work together. That's all I'm trying to say."

We descended a darkened staircase in silence and as my anger slid away, guilt replaced it. "I'm sorry, Deg."

He shrugged. "No worries. I do understand."

"You're right. I'm stuck in the past. But I'm willing to work on this...whatever we have together now."

"A partnership," he said with a reassuring smile.

I gave him a smile in return. "I like the sound of that."

Brock and Mandy argued playfully in front of us, both clearly the worse for wear but still lively enough to take jabs at each other. Suddenly I was glad they were in my court. I'd needed their help and they'd stepped up.

Like Deg.

I glanced up at him and found him watching me. Sighing, I shook my head. "And you're right about something else too. So many things are bothering me right now. Like, for example, the fact that Star was able to impersonate so many others. Like the fact that I'd really liked and trusted Posh…" My voice trailed off. I really had thought Posh and I could be friends. That loss made me sad.

He gave my shoulders a squeeze, holding the door for me and stepping back so I could exit the horrible building into a cool, sweetly scented night. "Star was apparently able to project herself to be whomever she chose. You thought you saw your ex. Others saw people they'd trusted when they looked at her." He frowned and I suddenly realized he might have seen someone too. "Who was it?" I asked.

Deg's gaze dropped sharply to mine, his sexy mouth tightening. "It doesn't matter. Just someone from my past."

A painful jolt speared me in the general vicinity of my heart and I realized it had come from him. My weariness deepened as the realization brought another on its heels. I'd bonded with a Witch. I was now, for all intents and purposes, his Familiar. It was something I'd never envisioned myself doing.

A quick sliver of regret tugged at me. But I pushed it away. I'd done what I had to do…for my family and my friends. I wouldn't regret it.

But I did need to figure out what to do with it.

I frowned up at him. "You knew it was Posh didn't you? When you first got here, you and Mandy kept exchanging glances like there was something you didn't want to tell me."

"Not really no. We found the cat's body outside." He

shook his head. "Seeing her dead terrified me. I thought you were gone too."

"Her body? I don't understand."

"I don't really understand it either. But it looks like your friend Posh wasn't the Demon. Star was just using her form to entice you literally into her web."

That made me feel a little better about my judgment. I'd really liked Posh. "She must have followed Tabby here…" I trailed off, feeling sad at the big cat's loss. Then I shook it off, saving it for when I was alone. "We need to talk about what's happened between us."

He nodded. "We will. We'll need to train and practice with the bond. I have some ideas…" He trailed off, giving me a look as we prepared to step into the barrier around Illusory Park. "And I'm sure you have some too. We'll make it work, LA."

I gave him a smile that I hoped didn't look too doubt-ful. For better or worse, Deg and I were bonded. We would face the future together. That prospect looked daunting for the moment. But there was also a great array of possibilities inherent with it. "I'm looking forward to it," I told him softly.

And in that moment I realized I was.

There was no going back. I stepped through the barrier, enjoying the swift blast of energy and the excited threads of magic that formed it. Everyone was back where they belonged. Thinking of Tabby and Posh I sighed. Almost everyone. I would mourn my lost friends by being a better Familiar. A better person. I'd become an asset to the people I cared about instead of a liability.

Deg dropped an arm around my shoulders as we

walked up the steps of my cozy home, heading for the golden light behind the leaded glass windows.

My life was falling back into place and going forward suddenly seemed much more exciting than ever before.

I decided it was a good time to be a magical Familiar.

A very good time.

ABOUT THE AUTHOR

USA Today Bestselling Author Sam Cheever writes romantic paranormal/fantasy and mystery/suspense, creating stories that celebrate the joy of love in all its forms. Known for writing great characters, snappy dialogue, and unique and exhilarating stories, Sam is the award-winning author of 50+ books and has been writing for over a decade under several noms de plume.

To learn more about Sam and her work, visit her at one of her online hotspots:

www.samcheever.com
samcheever@samcheever.com